For Dall..

a tale

Just Sand

THE
OPIATE
MURDERS

Justin Sand

 FriesenPress

Suite 300 - 990 Fort St
Victoria, BC, V8V 3K2
Canada

www.friesenpress.com

Copyright © 2021 by Justin Sand
First Edition — 2021

All rights reserved.

No part of this publication may be reproduced in any form, or by any means, electronic or mechanical, including photocopying, recording, or any information browsing, storage, or retrieval system, without permission in writing from FriesenPress.

ISBN
978-1-03-910529-4 (Hardcover)
978-1-03-910528-7 (Paperback)
978-1-03-910530-0 (eBook)

1. FICTION, CRIME

Distributed to the trade by The Ingram Book Company

This book is dedicated to Harm Reduction Workers,
a little less than a paramedic
but far above the angels.

Author's Note

I AM WRITING THIS BOOK BASED ON MY EXPERIENCE WORKING AS A HARM reduction worker in Victoria, B.C., Canada during 2020. I had already lived in the city for twelve years at the time. I went to work in the safe injection site on the 900 block of Pandora in January 2020. I never wanted to write this story; this story chose me. I was working at a makeshift homeless shelter when I discovered a man sitting beside a girl who was dying beside him of an overdose. He was tapping his foot. I asked him if she was okay, and he told me she was just fucked up. I rolled her over, and her face was white, and her lips were blue. I saved the girl's life, and he ran way. He had been involved in an overdose one hour before with another person in the same exact spot. It took extraordinary measures to save that person as well. He had sat there once everyone had left, and he did it again. It was his dope that he had made at home. He had a history of doping girls up and assaulting them. I reported him to everyone I knew, but nothing was done. One day I watched him walk up to my place of work and sit down a hundred yards from the door. He knew nobody was looking for him. Maybe now somebody will.

1

THE PAVEMENT WAS MOIST AND COLD UNDER HIS FEET AS HE WALKED after a long, torrential downpour. Rosy stood in her usual spot scared at first, but then she softened to his image as he got closer. Rosy couldn't wear her glasses at work even if she had any. The streets were still empty from fear of a looming pandemic that had yet to materialize.

"Hey girl, how's it going?" he said as he pulled his pipe from his inside pocket.

"Nothing's going," Rosy said as her eyes fixated on his pipe.

"You want a hit?" he asked as he pulled his lighter from his pocket.

Rosy hesitated for a second and ran down the list of potential threats in her head. The urge overtook the need for safety as she reached out and took the pipe. She knew the man as Dax, but she didn't know him well. She didn't know a lot of men well, but there she was. She hadn't had a john in hours, and the feeling in her stomach just kept sinking lower and lower. She took the pipe and put it to her lips as Dax lit the end and looked over her shoulder.

There it was, that familiar feeling coming on. It started with the taste, and before she knew it that feeling of fading engulfed her. She was free: free of the street, the cops, the johns, and all those regrets. She leaned against the wall and began to slide down it. She welcomed it. She relied on it. Down was all she lived for now. She was gone. As she gasped her last breaths, his eyes darted back and forth looking for witnesses. His heart was pounding. With every death came anxiety, but then after, pure bliss and purpose. He longed for purpose, and as he watched her face turn white and her lips turn dark blue, he found his. She was no longer gasping periodically. Nobody heard the death rattle but him.

He took a deep breath, removed the pipe that was gripped in her hand, and walked off into the night. He never looked back. He imagined every siren he heard after that was coming for her. His work was done, and now he could sit back and enjoy the bliss that came with every mention of another opiate death that had happened somewhere down off Pandora Street.

2

KATE WOKE UP TO THE SOUND OF A BLARING ALARM. 5:15 A.M. WAS A TIME she used to dread, but now she just pulled herself out of bed with all her might and used the "why" of coffee as her excuse. A lit cigarette and coffee would prime her for whatever came after that. She thought back to her days in university when she could wake up at noon if she wanted. She wondered where those days had gone.

She was twenty-five now. She stood in front of the mirror and put on the least amount of concealer she could manage without drawing attention to herself. She got enough of that already. Her grandma had told her when she was growing up that "beautiful things don't beg for attention" and she always believed that. She *was* beautiful, not in the kind of way that is despised, but in the kind of way that is understood. Her blueish-green eyes shimmered in the mirror as she combed her strawberry-blonde hair straight enough. She usually dressed down, and she had even found a coat that dipped down to the back of her knees.

It was still pitch black outside when she walked to the bus stop. The streets were abandoned. It was rare to have anyone on the bus with her nowadays. The news of the pandemic sweeping across the globe had shut down all the businesses around her work. Kate couldn't even get a coffee from the McDonald's across the street because only the drive-thru was open. As she turned the corner on to Pandora, she approached the sight that had once terrified her. It looked like a sea of tents parted by the street running through it. Tents filled the grassy islands that hugged the edges of Pandora Street and also were erected against the building. She recognized every face, and only said "morning" to those that looked at her. She passed by a van that was handing out coffee and doughnuts to the homeless on her way to the front door of the safe injection site where she worked.

The front door was blocked by tarps, so she peered over one of the openings and assessed whether or not she could barter for entrance. She said, "Good morning," in a probing tone and waited for a response. "Not yet," she heard come from deep in the darkness under the tarp. She decided to go around to the back. She sidestepped the human feces all along the side driveway on her way around back. The looming pandemic had left the homeless without bathrooms or showers to use, so they were forced to go wherever would afford them enough dignity. The alley on the side of the building turned out to be the place.

The twenty-foot-high gate swung open, and Kate proceeded to the back door of the facility. She opened the door after swiping her key card and was quickly engulfed in bright halogen light. She put her lunch in the staff room and made coffee in the chill room located behind the gallery. Once the coffee began to percolate, she stepped through the sliding door and into the gallery. Before her stood ten stainless steel booths with large mirrors in each one and a large exhaust fan above. The sight gleamed with sparkling metallic disinfection because each booth was cleaned relentlessly after each use and every night after close.

They opened the door at 7:30 a.m., so she used the next thirty minutes to check the shift reports from the previous day and all the other work-related chatter that seemed to grow in her inbox. She poured herself a coffee and welcomed the paramedic, Andrea, scheduled that Monday. Andrea went into the staff room and put on her uniform. The Gate was the name of their safe injection service, it was staffed by three to five harm reduction workers and a paramedic. The service was run by the ambulance service and a few different non-profits. The other harm reduction staff started to show up shortly after. The staff was a mixture of hipster-punk-type men with the occasional heavy metal affiliate, and the women were a mix between the girl next door and the lead actress from your favourite witch movie. That was only the beginning of the personas that worked there because there was a number of self-identifying types who made their own categories and took no shit from anyone.

"Should I check the back door?" Gary asked as he walked the hallway towards the back door and chill room.

"Try your luck," Kate said as she sat scrolling on her phone, savoring the last sip of her coffee.

"Another fifteen minutes," Gary said after trying to open the back door that was conveniently located in the front and just twenty feet from the front door. He proceeded to go into the front office located directly in the middle of it all. The facility was shaped like a U. When the door opened, a client would register and come into the waiting room through a second set of doors and wait. If there was room inside, a big sliding door would then let them in the gallery. Once inside, they used what they had brought in, and when they were done, they went into the chill room for observation, if they wanted. Most people just walked through the chill room and out the door. It was 7:30 a.m. and Kate started to hear the yelling that was starting over the people blocking the front door. The day was about to begin.

3

DET. GLORIA DIXON PULLED UP TO AN ADDRESS JUST OFF DOUGLAS AT about 8:30 a.m. that morning. She had been a detective for eleven years in this city, and it was starting to wear on her. She looked out over the scene and recognized most of the faces there from other scenes just like this one. She wondered if this was all there was as she fumbled through a few emails on the computer and logged her time in. She took a quick glance in the rear-view mirror to check her makeup, but she pretended to be checking the perimeter. It was an old trick she learned in her first year. "Make everything look official" was what she had learned while she wore the badge.

She stepped out of the car and took the control that was afforded her by her experience and her rank. She talked a moment with the officers guarding the perimeter and then moved along down the line of hands until she was standing square to the deceased. "What am I looking at here?" she asked the nearest sergeant.

A man looked up at her, shook her hand, and then proceeded. "This is Rose Donaldson, known to many on the block as just 'straight Rose'. She is a known prostitute and drug trafficker. She was found here this morning, just as you see her, leaned up against this wall just out of sight of Douglas Street. Looks like an opiate overdose judging by the complexion of the deceased. No witnesses."

Gloria knelt down and looked at Rose's face and then looked around on the ground. "Where's the pipe?" she asked looking down the line at the other officers.

"Well, that's the only part we can't figure out. We got no signs that this was intravenous, but we also have no pipe," he said looking at her with an estranged glance.

Gloria knew this story all too well; it had become common to her ever since she started working major crimes. "The deceased smoked with someone else either here or somewhere else and succumbed to the dope in that person's presence or just after they left. Some people just don't want to deal with an overdose," Gloria said, just as she had said a million times, it felt. The last five years had become especially bad because of fentanyl. Gloria reflected how powerful this synthetic opiate was – even in small doses. In the last ten years, the drug had led to an overwhelming amount of opiate deaths in this city and all over the world. Gloria looked around the body once more before returning to the perimeter. Once she returned to the car, she heard a call come in – the same call that got her to this site. She turned the keys and drove up to the 900 block of Pandora.

4

KATE STARTED UP FRONT AFTER THE DOORS HAD BEEN CLEARED, CHECKing people into the site. They stated their "site name", which wasn't their real name at all. Names like "Paul F" and "John A" were common names. Kate entered the names into the system on the computer and alerted the staff inside the unit that there were participants waiting. The sliding doors to the gallery opened, and men in construction clothes shuffled in to get their first fix in. Ever since the safe injection site had opened, there had been a decrease in overdose deaths averaging seven a week. Safe injection sites were designated an essential service because of this.

It was an amazing reality to discover for Kate. Here, this place sat, in the middle of downtown and it held one of the city's biggest secrets. Kate learned the secret in her first week: People from every walk of life use heroin before they go to work. Sometimes men came in suits. That day was no different, these people used quick and headed off to work. The girls would come in, fix, and then they would go sleep off a long night out in the streets. Lots of the girls just came in to sleep during the day and were afforded this luxury by management because the risk of being raped was so prevalent at night.

Kate sat at her kiosk and marveled at the red and blue lights that lit up her glazed windows. She left her post and went out the front door to look. Once outside, Kate was confronted by the sight of an ambulance and police cars. Since the impending pandemic, the government had handed out tents to people on the block. The tents were scattered all over the block now, and she could see participants running from tent to tent like cats. She watched the police standing outside one tent exclusively. "What's going on," Kate asked one of the onlookers.

"They pulled a body out of that tent a couple minutes ago," the man said as he took a drag off his smoke.

"What?!" Kate exclaimed.

5

EVER SINCE GLORIA HAD BEEN A LITTLE GIRL, SHE WANTED TO BE POLICE. Her dad, Mel, was a detective in Vancouver before they moved to Victoria. He had continued at the police department, becoming a captain and retiring with honors. Gloria's mother had passed early in her life, so she was drawn to the group early on. Gloria loved the team of people he worked with; they all took turns bringing up Gloria. The barbecues and baseball games lit up all her memories as a child. She would sit around and listen to the glory and tragedy of the job. It always seemed more interesting than fashion and gossip, which was the staple of other girls' families she knew. Who was dating whom? Who was working where? What was really going on in that house? It never appealed to her. She wanted to chase bad guys and rescue victims. She wanted "the life" as they called it.

When Gloria pulled up to the scene, she was met by an army of people: Fire, ambulance, auxiliary cops, and some of her people. When she got the call to come to the 900 block of Pandora, she knew it had to be big. The news crews always got to these locations fastest. The public was very interested with what went on there and not because they were concerned for the people there. The place was hated by every entitled voter driving to work in the morning.

She stepped out and approached the perimeter cops first. Once she had been filled in, she walked slowly towards the tent, taking in every detail she could. She glanced at one of the officers standing nearest her and asked what they had. The man turned to her and walked her around the tent and then towards an ambulance. She was informed that early morning tent checks had revealed a dead body inside the tent: one man, possibly overdosed, given the state of the deceased on discovery. Gloria looked at one of the officers and, holding her hand to her nose, asked, "Is there something special down here or does it smell like raw sewage?"

One of the officers motioned up the street and said, "Everyone has been pushed out into the street. No bathrooms, no showers. It's been going on for at least two weeks now."

She looked around and noticed way more garbage than usual. "What's with all the garbage?" Gloria asked.

"The city workers refuse to come down here and take the garbage," he said.

"And we're expecting a pandemic?" Gloria said as she rolled her eyes. Gloria stared at the body for a moment and took in the scene. The body hadn't been moved and was in an arched position. She knew when a person overdoses when they are lying down, their head tilts back, their lips turn blue, and their face turns white. If the person was sitting, their head can be found tilted forward. The needle was still in his arm. Gloria motioned to forensics, and they gave her the "nod", which meant that it was a lot of paperwork but no real crime.

Gloria covered her face as she walked back to the car. She noticed that none of the homeless had been raised from their tents. Usually in the morning, the police and city workers would raise people, clear them off the sidewalk, and then sanitize and take the garbage. She remembered doing it when she was a beat cop. Some of the cops loved it. She never felt comfortable with it. The idea of waking someone in a tent on the street was soul crushing. The idea of where they go from there was too much to fathom. Gloria realized in that moment that this situation was going to get worse by the day. She filed her report back in the office (her car), stating the conditions that she found deplorable. She wondered if anyone would ever read it.

6

DAX SAT IN HIS APARTMENT AND WATCHED THE MORNING NEWS. HE waited patiently with his hands in his lap, watching for it. Finally, it came. As they mentioned the overdoses, his eyes dilated, he exhaled, and his head dropped forward and his eyes watered. In the moments following the report, he felt his purpose illuminated for all to see but none to know but him. He was getting rid of the lazy, the useless, the whores, and the unemployed. He was the one who would do what the public couldn't or didn't have the guts to do. He was the chosen one. As he sat there, he listened. As he sat there, he waited. He waited for them to say the words. It was never the same, but the message was clear: They had nothing, and they weren't looking either. Nobody was going to miss another junkie hooker.

KATE SAT IN HER BOOTH AT THE FRONT DOOR OF THE SITE AND GATHERED information from the people who checked in. Some had been on the block all night and couldn't believe Brandon was dead. He was the last person anybody would expect, it seemed. Kate knew Brandon and had dealt with him often. Brandon had been kind and generous in his dealings with the staff. He was appreciated for that. He seemed to keep his own council and stay out of most of the drama. He had been sleeping outside in a tent like everyone else since the pandemic restrictions took place.

He would be missed, and there was a quietness to the block and the site following the news. Death on the block was felt by everyone; it wasn't isolated. Kate figured out early on that these people were like family. They fought with each other, corrected each other, and most importantly, they took care of each other. Kate watched people take the news, and she felt their pain. She cleared a tear from her eye as she watched a young woman cry and stomp her feet in outrage. The people down here didn't hide their emotions; they felt every emotion. Kate had no doubt that this wouldn't be the only overdose, but hopefully if they did their jobs and got lucky, there wouldn't be any deaths. She was proud of the fact that since the safe injection site had opened there hadn't been one overdose death inside. She couldn't protect them from the night, but she could offer them a safe harbour during the day.

Just then, a client named Gang Star came in to get a straight shooter and informed Kate of the overdose. "I know it happened in the night," Kate said.

"It happened down off Douglas too. Rosie's dead," he said as he stepped out the doors and on to the street.

Kate was shocked as she took a walk into the office and reported the news to Catherine, the supervisor. "Fuck," Catherine said as she stared down at the ground. Straight Rosie had been a long-time client of the site and had many friends there. Kate took her break after that; it was only 10:00 a.m.

8

IN THE DAYS FOLLOWING THE OVERDOSES, THE PANDEMIC RESTRICTIONS began to tighten. The booths at the site went from ten booths, with the adjacent chill room that could fit at least twenty, to five booths with three allowed in chill. Kate started to fear again what she would see when she turned that corner on Vancouver Street and walked down Pandora. The smell was getting worse, and the people on the block were getting more and more afraid. Kate would come into work and find out that there had been stabbings and beatings of people on the block. Targeted purges for old beefs and trifles, no doubt. The police had stopped patrolling, and if you were caught for a crime, you were quickly released from jail because the pandemic restrictions made it impossible to process new cases.

The overdose rate began to rise with the level of anxiety perpetrated by every news outlet. Anywhere outside of the block, the pandemic was manageable because citizens could shelter in place. On the block, there was nowhere to shelter in place. That reality was held on every face out there. They all thought they were going to die. Every morning the tents were still, and nobody was moving. The amount of booths open went from five to three, and then to one.

Kate was turning away dozens of people every hour. She was sick to her stomach from all the terror that was thrown her way by the clients who couldn't understand why they couldn't use any of the services on the block. Since they were turning so many away, the amount of overdoses on the street started to rise. Now, instead of being able to supervise people as they used, the staff were called outside by people banging on the door to tell them there was an overdose on the street.

That meant Kate and the other staff had to run out the door and start loading shots into a person without any of the information about (how long they had been down, how much they used, what time). It was the epitome of their normal job on steroids. Sometimes they would run a block and climb a fence to rescue a person that was already dead. Kate was blown away when some of these people came back to life. One of Kate's managers had a heart attack and went on leave.

Kate watched as the people became more desperate and the street got more contaminated. Kate reported the conditions outside to the newspaper. She reported that they had stopped disinfecting the street and taking the garbage. She explained that these protocols were there for a reason. The conditions there now were fuel for a pandemic. And there were even worse realities from Kate's point of view. What about other diseases like staph infection, sepsis, and typhoid to name a few? The people out in the street were no longer able to shower or go to the bathroom inside. They had created the perfect conditions for disease out there.

The safe injection site received its commands to close on April 3. That month saw the highest rate of overdose deaths since the beginning of the overdose crisis back in 1991. On Kate's last day, she went home and balled her eyes out at the thought of all those people out there left to die. She couldn't help them; everyone was too busy saving themselves from a pandemic that had yet to materialize. Not one person either working or homeless on the street was sick. Forty-four cases would be reported between the months of March and Sept 2020. It was a nightmare because of the shutdown.

Kate spent that month at home even though some of her co-workers set up outside the safe injection site. Kate thought the government should have to come down to work out in the street, she believed this was all a bad idea. Why close down and move everyone to camps? Why couldn't they just block off the ends of the street and keep all the services open? The whole place could be a house. Nobody down there was social distancing because this was their home.

Kate sat home and listened to the Canadian version – banging pots and pans as if at a hockey game – of what other quarantining countries were doing to recognize healthcare workers. She thought about all the healthcare workers patting each other on the back with empty hospitals, while down on the block, people were being treated like animals and dying in their own shit. This was systematic genocide of the homeless population, and it made her sick to be part of this country. She felt guilty about not working down there, but she couldn't support the genocide. A few weeks later, the city started clearing Pandora and pushing people into camps across the city. Many would die; far more would live to tell the tale.

Overdose and death were a constant in those days as spring began. Many bodies would lie in tents undiscovered for up to eleven days in the camps.

9

DAX FIXED A TOURNIQUET AROUND HIS ARM AND DID A SMASH OF HEROIN. He sat back and let it take hold of him. His eyes rolled back, and his body went numb he sailed away to that place he had found all those years ago. Dax had been using junk since he was sixteen. It was the only way to stay sane out there on the streets. Dax had been in a car accident when he was younger, so he had always been crippled. The pain of being just out of reach of all things athletic stung almost as bad as his actual pain. It was hard for him to grow up out here with a limp like that and a cane.

He played it up to be much worse than it was though. He learned that early on, if he played the possum, he could gain the upper hand. It started in fights. When someone attacked him, he would cower, letting the person grow tired, and then he would attack. He played up his injuries, making himself appear more feeble and useless than he was so he could attack with surprise. Girls were put off by him. He had to pay for it if he was ever lonely, but he couldn't always afford it. He started to make his own dope early on. It gave him some prestige at first but slowly turned him into a dope pusher. He sought the power of the street and all it could offer. He would dope the girls up now and take what he wanted. When he was young, it seemed so innocent, when he was young it seemed so tame, but now that he had grown older and his hair started to frost, he looked sinister when he approached girls on the block. Word had got out a few years past about his behavior with one of the girls, and he was chased off the block now. That is when he turned. It was then that he decided to become the Reaper.

The Reaper thought these girls out here were nothing but the walking dead. When the average citizen saw one of these girls, they didn't know where to look out of shame, and would do anything so the girl wouldn't approach them. These souls needed to be collected. The Reaper collected souls inside his glass pipe. When it was time, he would creep up to them and take them out of this cruel world. He was doing what the families and public couldn't. Fentanyl was the perfect ether for their transformation. So subtle were its qualities but how powerful its consequences. All you needed was the perfect balance between benzos and pure fentanyl, and they were gone. To die how they lived sucking their soul through the hole in the pipe.

The first time you kill someone it is terrifying, but the first time you get away with it, now that's transcendence. Dax had found his purpose in the first news broadcast. "Today a young woman was found dead out in the street in the morning hours, another casualty of the growing opiate epidemic." He lived to hear about his work on the news. He went to all the wakes and funerals of all his victims too. Dax was a regular shoulder to cry on. 'And why not?' he thought. Why shouldn't they get to meet their taker?

The days seemed to drag on and on, but when night finally came, Dax geared up to make a pass through the streets of pain and wasting. He chose the loaners. He chose the mentally ill. He chose the ones that nobody would miss. He was always careful. He carried different products for different people. If there was a witness watching, he would give away his good dope; but if nobody was around, he would load the pipe with the rope. They would hang there for a minute and then off they would go, deep into that grave they had been digging for all those years. He wasn't a murderer; he was a liberator. He was the one that had the guts to send these trauma ridden souls on to the next place. He sent them there through his pipe.

Nobody investigated these crimes because they were made in the same place as the addiction. Nobody wants to know how these people got this way; that's why they don't miss them when they are gone. The end justifies the means. Dax was doing the city's dirty work, and he knew he wasn't the only one. Dax had grown up watching people take the hot shot. The street takes care of its own.

10

KATE RECEIVED A TEXT FROM ONE OF THE NON-PROFITS SHE HAD WORKED for in the past, asking her if she wanted to come back to work inside in May. In an attempt to mitigate the damage done by closing the safe injection site and putting people into camps, the city had started buying up hotels to house the vulnerable populations of the city. One of those ideas was to use "the Arena" as a shelter, and Kate was asked if she wanted to work there. Kate looked around her cagey apartment with her clothes strung everywhere and the sink full of dirty dishes and thought of *him*. He had been gone so long now that it was like he wasn't real. It was like she had imagined him. Then she would feel his cold skin under her fingertips. She agreed to go back to work. Anything to get her away from that feeling and back to a place that made sense.

The arena was exactly what it sounded like: It was a hockey stadium turned into a makeshift homeless shelter. Imagine fifty-foot ceilings for an entrance, a hockey rink for the beds, and you've made a great start. When Kate got there, she quickly noticed that the booths for consumption were just up against the wall to the left of the entrance when you walked in; there was no privacy. She was told that they would be building a consumption room the next day. Apparently, they had done this at all the hotels they had bought or rented. Kate recognized some faces but didn't really know anyone except for the people she worked with. She had worked for this company for a while, but she had never worked exclusively for it, she had always just worked as one staff amongst another company who ran the site. Executive was actually running the site and the people she worked with were thrilled. She would be working ten-hour shifts for four days with three days off. This was a break from her two seven-hour and two fourteen-hour shifts she usually worked.

The clientele was pretty sporadic in that she only provided services for maybe ten percent of the people there. Mostly people just used in their pods (which made sense); they weren't willing to let a stranger watch them use when they could lie in their bed. She saw the odd person but mostly handed out gear, walked around, and tried not to fall asleep. There hadn't been any overdoses yet at the Arena, and there wasn't any reason to expect any, given the fact that there were so few people here compared to what she was used to. She passed the time getting to know the security and the people from the other non-profit that ran the site. Most of the security were Eastern immigrants, and they didn't understand the culture of these people. In a lot of foreign countries, Kate learned, the homeless and addicted populations were rounded up and shot. She tried her best to explain that these people were in a transitional stage in their lives and recovering from trauma. She insisted with stabilization they would all use less and commit less acts of violence.

She would occasionally see someone she knew from Pandora, but she wouldn't really recognize them. The person would have gained weight and be walking around talking to people. She only knew the skinny, desperate version of this person. She was used to people fighting their way into her unit and using as much as they could for as long as they could. She realized that what she was witnessing was a miracle. The people she knew were completely changing right before her eyes. She had always known it could be possible, but she never thought a pandemic would create the conditions for it to occur. Day in and day out, she watched people she knew transform.

They didn't use her service very much; they found other things to do like complaining about the food or the living conditions. There were no doors inside the arena – or walls for that matter – so people's stuff could be stolen at any time, and it was. Stuff was constantly being stolen, all the time so there was always drama in the site. "Some things did carry over from Pandora," Kate thought. She hadn't got used to people having all their stuff stolen but she had learned to live with it. At first, she had hated everyone she suspected, but after a while she noticed that they all did it. It seemed like it was all part of it. She had seen it happen so many times to so many people that it became normal for her. The weeks went by like that for her, ten-hour days inside a makeshift consumption site, under those halogen ballasts.

Kate's non-profit was unique, and depending on your perspective, it was either very good or very bad. Kate was ambivalent to her circumstances because she was a clean person, who did not use drugs anymore, but she was working within a collective of people who were all still using drugs. The Executive staffed their sites with actively using employees. Needless to say, they had a lot of people late and constant no shows. So, she was usually working short-handed in some capacity. On the day in question, she was short-handed which meant Kate was inside, and one person was outside watching the consumption tent where people smoked narcotics behind a partition that just happened to be located right next to the police station. Most people were outside smoking side and doing dragons (crystal meth, heroin/fentanyl). Kate liked the security of working inside a building while the other employees usually smoked cigarettes, so they liked to be outside, which worked out well, as long as nothing happened. When you are supposed to have three people and you only have two on shift you are constantly exposed.

At about 3:30 p.m., Kate decided to get a drink from the corner store that was a five-minute walk from her work, just across a parking lot. When she started walking back, all she could see was a fire truck, ambulance, and a bunch of cops. Her pace began to quicken, but then she slowed to take in the sight. To her left stood onlookers and a parked ambulance that was in front of the fire truck. Just a little ways down on the left were nine cops standing off to one side against the wall; it was shift change and a bunch of them had just accumulated out there beside their station. To the right of them, Kate could see the ambulance people down on their knees working on a guy who had no shirt on and tattoos all over him. He had an oxygen mask on his face and wasn't moving. To the right of them and partially blocking the view was a great big column with a man standing over the body. He stood out to her as a man who had been hanging around outside of the partition all day.

Kate asked her co-worker Kurt what had happened. He told her he had watched the guy go down smoking a dragon and then realized that he didn't have any Narcan on him. As Kate had the only key to the consumption room, Kurt had to run to the site office to get some. Kate's eyes went wide, and she felt a huge dose of failure and shame wash over her. 'Sometimes it only takes five minutes to change the course of a life' She had taken the keys with her, not thinking that anything would happen in five minutes. Kate looked around for something to hang on to, but all she could see was him.

"Can you pass me my cane?" the man leaning against the column for support asked the paramedics as she passed. Kate went inside and quickly filled three shots of Narcan and put it in her kit. If she knew anything, it was that if one person goes down from an overdose, there is bound to be another. She learned that at the safe consumption site where they often had multiple overdoses at the same time. Kate knew it was better to have and not need than to need and not have. Some people pre-loaded a shot every morning just in case.

A short while later, Kurt left for his break and a new guy came in for his shift and went inside. Kate decided to work outside till Kurt got back. As she walked back and forth across the parking lot, she realized that she had made a huge mistake. If only she had given Kurt the keys, he wouldn't have had to run to the office and make the company look incompetent. She canvassed the bushes along the edge of the parking lot and made another sweep. 'At least they got that guy back on his feet and took him to the hospital,' Kate thought.

It had taken eight shots of Narcan. Kurt had mentioned that in all his years of doing this, the most he had ever given anyone was three. As Kate walked back to the scene of the overdose, she noticed the guy with the cane was sitting there with a girl she recognized from inside. Kate walked over to the police station and then doubled back past them just in time to see him lighting the girl's pipe. Kate walked around the partition and noticed some broken glass inside it. She got security to let her into the building so she could get a broom and a dustpan. When she checked on her co-worker inside, he was asleep. She shook her head and went outside to clean up the glass. As soon as she began sweeping, she heard *the sound*.

The first time Kate had heard that sound they were responding to an overdose in the street outside the safe consumption site on Pandora. A man had been found in the bushes up against a building. When they got around the gate and down the path that led to him, they found a man with dark blue lips and a sheer white face lying on the ground. He looked dead. They started loading up the Narcan shots while the point woman practiced rescue breaths on him. As Kate loaded up her shot, she saw the man go from not breathing at all to gasping a gargled intense breath that shrieked to the depths of his soul. It was the epitome of a death rattle. He wasn't breathing on his own yet, so Kate couldn't tell if that was either his first breath towards life or his last. The man finally came to after three shots of Narcan. Then he did another typical thing of an opiate overdose, he tried to leave the scene. He was detained by nearby police who yelled at him, "You were dead! And now you got some place to be?! Wait for the ambulance!"

The death rattle shook Kate from her monotonous chore, and she turned left and right trying to figure out from where the sound was coming. She ran to the inside corner of the partition and pulled back the cover. She found herself looking into the eyes of a man whose head had swung around to meet her urgency. He wasn't the source of the sound, but she noticed that the chair beside him was empty. Confused, she put the cover back and walked back to her broom and dustpan. In that moment, she looked back to her right and through the refuse that lined the inside bottom of the partition and saw two legs sticking out. Kate panicked and ran around the outside of the partition to where the man sat. "Hey, is she okay?!" Kate demanded urgently.

"Ya she's fine, She's just fucked up," he said forcefully.

"Are you sure?" Kate asked as she pulled at the body.

"Watch her arm," the man said as Kate pulled her free of the fence line where her head had been stuffed into the corner.

The woman's face was white, and her lips were blue. Kate could see the pipe gripped in her hand as she rolled her over. "Go get everybody!" Kate yelled at him. Kate quickly fumbled through her kit for the shots of Narcan, gave the woman one in each leg, and waited for signs of life. Kate didn't hesitate to give her the third shot remembering how many shots it had taken for the last guy to stand up.

The security guard asked Kate if she needed anything and she said "get the staff from inside with the oxygen" as Kate applied stimulation to the woman's shoulders watching for the light to return in the her eyes. Just as the site staff came rushing up, Kate heard the woman's voice say, "Hi." Kate exhaled deeply as she took the oxygen mask from the site staff and put it over the woman's face. Kate waited until she saw the twinkle in her eye before she asked her the standard questions.

"Do you know where you are?"

"Yes."

"Have you ever overdosed before?"

"Yes."

"Do you want an ambulance?"

"No."

The woman quickly went back inside the building after that. The security guy told Kate that the guy who had been with her had taken off.

"That was the same guy from the first overdose!" Kate yelled.

11

'FUCKING CUNT! THAT GIRL WAS MINE!' DAX SCREAMED INSIDE HIS HEAD as he made his way across Douglas and off into Rock Bay. 'My pipe is gone. All those souls are in the palm of that junkie bitch's hand. I must go back soon. When? Soon!' he said to himself, as he made his way into his basement apartment. He slammed the door and pulled all the blinds.

There in the dark he began to cry. 'It was so perfect,' he thought. It was the ultimate execution. It was the ultimate prize. Two souls and right in front of the police station; the plan was so close. If it wasn't for that stupid Executive fuck, I would have had the first one. I gave him enough dope to kill a small village. When he stood up, I was shocked. They took them from me! And that stupid cunt girl, I had that junkie bitch in the pipe. She was gone and then that stupid bitch ruined everything. I must go back. She has the vessel, the pipe. I must go back. But when?' he asked himself. 'Soon,' he answered.

'It was the perfect stage,' he lamented. 'I was going to show them all. I was going to show all those spectators in all those buildings surrounding that place, and even the police themselves, how it's done. No more making it easy for them. No more unemployed paradise.' He sobbed and held himself tight there in the dark. He would head out as soon as it got dark and get his vessel back. No junkie bitch was going to hold what he had worked so hard for. He would wait. In the shadows, and far from sight, he would wait for his opportunity, and he would take what was his.

12

KATE HAD PROBABLY TOLD THE STORY A DOZEN TIMES BEFORE THE NIGHT was over. When Kurt got back, she told him the story. Kurt's eyes got wide and said, "That guy tried to get me to stop working on the first guy." Kate and Kurt shook their heads in disbelief. In all the time they had been working they had never witnessed anything like this. Nobody stays around after and overdose. Nobody ignores a death rattle right beside them when it can be heard fifteen feet away. He was getting off on watching her die. Who stands over a body of someone they gave poisonous dope to like it was nothing watching them receive shot after shot and then stays around after and gives that same dope to someone new?

The site told Kate it took 13 shots of Narcan and a nasal (equivalent to 10 shots 4.0 of Narcan) in the middle of it to get the first guy up. She told people inside the unit and started to hear the tale of the man who had been outside all day. One of the clients fixed a needle into his arm as he talked to Kate – which was not anything out of the ordinary for either of them. "You know, it's funny you say that about the guy because a couple years ago I heard the same kind of story about him. Dax had a bunch of girls run him off the block a couple years ago because he was fucking with them when they were passed out," the guy said as he did a smash and clenched his teeth with the strap in his mouth.

Kate was fascinated and relieved by people who smashed crystal meth. They never seemed to overdose or pass out. 'Easy money,' she always thought.

As 9:00 p.m. rolled around, Kate said her goodbyes to the staff and headed home for three days off. Kate always felt crazy for the first day she was off. She could feel herself negotiating the grief and trauma that was foisted upon her day in and day out in the unit. The images would come to her as she lay in her bed. She felt dead inside at first – like she was an empty theatre where ghouls and goblins came to improve their craft. Slowly, her power would come back with sleep and food. She would watch Netflix or the latest new release and cry. She would cry for no apparent reason it would seem, but she would be happy when it was done.

The days would usually slide by without a trace, but not this time. She couldn't get that image out of her head. Dax staring at her with that look, the same look he had had all day. Evil just hiding there in plain view. It changed her. She had to tell the police. Every time she heard an ambulance, she imagined it was him killing another person. She couldn't stop him alone. Monday morning, she would do something. Monday morning, she would go into the police station and report this. 'They must have had a camera pointed over there,' she thought. 'It was right in front of them.'

The days off slipped away, and on her last day off, Monday morning, she went to the police station. The sign outside read: "No Entry Due to Pandemic protocol" with a number to call. She walked away from the front door and listened to the phone ring. On the fourth ring, the dispatch answered: "Any Police dispatch," the woman said.

"Hello, this is Kate Reynolds. I work in the building next to you," she said, getting the tone of her voice balanced.

"Yes, what do you have to report?" the woman said with a sound of annoyance in her voice.

Kate wasn't expecting to have to report this verbally. She thought she would be able to write it down. She was expecting time. She was expecting patience. Kate took a deep breath and just let her have it. "You know that you had the two overdoses within an hour of each other next door on Friday?"

"Yes," the woman said with a tinge of confusion.

"Well, on Friday I stepped out to get a drink, and on my way back, I could see that all the king's horses were here – fire, ambulance, and a bunch of police. When I was walking back, I could see a guy standing in the middle of the scene. I mean, he was *right* in the middle, asking for his cane to be passed to him. Anyways, it took thirteen shots of Narcan to get the guy up and a nasal in the middle. Then everybody leaves because nothing clears a party like an overdose. So, I load up three shots, because when one person goes down, there are bound to be others. One of my co-workers was on a break, so I was outside.

"I start walking back and forth across the parking lot, and I notice that the man who was in the middle of the overdose scene is still sitting over on the outside of the partition. So, I continue to walk back and forth, and after a few rounds, I notice that one of the girls has come outside of the arena, and now she is sitting with him. Now, on another round, I look over and I see him lighting a pipe for her. As I don't judge our residents, I just continue walking to the front door when I notice that there is some broken glass inside the partition that they are on the outside of. I run inside to get a broom for the glass and start sweeping it up when I hear the sound."

Kate let out her impersonation of a death rattle. A gnawing, gargling sound.

The dispatch, now very annoyed, responds "Yes, I know the sound."

Kate caught her breath and continued. "So I run over to the inside corner of the partition and pull the curtain back, and all I see is him sitting beside an empty chair. He looks back at me with a look that I can't describe. I don't know, maybe fear. I then step away and go back to my dustpan and ask myself, 'What was that?' Then, all of a sudden, I look to my right and I see it – her legs sticking out from some debris that is on the inside of the tent. I only see it because the partition is skirted, and you can see out the bottom foot of the partition.

"'Oh fuck,' I say as I run around the outside of the partition and come upon them. He is in the chair and she is on the ground right beside him. 'Hey, is she okay?!' I ask.

"'Ya, she's fine. She's just fucked up,' he says.

"'Are you sure?' I ask as I start pulling her away from the inside corner of the partition and the wall. Her lips were dark blue, and her face was white. I tell him to get everyone, and I quickly give her two shots," Kate said.

"Gave her two shots of what?" the dispatch interrupted.

"Narcan, .4 shots," Kate said, astonished that she was being questioned. She didn't expect to be interrupted let alone interrogated.

"Well, you need to be specific," the dispatch says with anxiety.

Kate continued in her story not knowing really where she was. "So, I wait a minute or so, and I just give her the other one. Just as the site people came with the oxygen and I was going to tell them to call the ambulance, the woman says, 'Hi.'"

The dispatch interrupted again. and says, "is she a resident there?"

"Yes," Kate said.

"Would she even want to talk to us about something that happened to her when she was high?" the dispatch asks disparagingly.

"She didn't even know where she was," Kate returns.

"Well, I don't even know if we can do anything if she doesn't know what happened. Would she even be willing to talk to us about what happened?" she said dismissively.

"Well, I was there, and I can tell you." Kate answers sternly.

"It's up to her if she is willing to charge anyone," the dispatch returns.

Kate continued talking and was quickly interrupted again.

"Sorry, I appreciate the story and everything, but we are supposed to keep this line open because of the pandemic, so if you could just get to the point?" she said forcefully.

Kate took a deep breath and just let the words come out. "I think this guy was trying to kill these two people," she said as she exhaled.

"Why didn't you report this before?" the dispatch accused.

Kate suddenly felt guilt pang away in her chest, and she fought back. "I did, the site has this all documented plus the security company, I just thought, after thinking about it all weekend, that I should report it to you guys too." She felt shaky. How could this be the response she was getting?

"Do you have names of the people involved? Are they residents?" dispatch asked again with annoyance.

"Only one person was a resident," Kate said.

"Well, get the name of the resident and the others involved and call back. We can't do anything until we have the names," dispatch answered.

The Opiate Murders

Kate hung up...

Kate was full of anxiety and fear as she walked towards Chinatown. She felt displaced from all reality. She couldn't believe how dismissive they were of something so callous. Kate played back every moment. Then the thought came to her like a forest fire in a high wind. 'This is the perfect climate to do this. The Cops won't even let you in the building. Someone could literally kill at will because people care even less than they usually do.'

'The public barely cares about these people on a good day,' Kate reflected, 'but now, now they can systematically ignore all of it.' She was reminded of a story she had heard about a serial killer who went on a killing spree in England during World War Two. It was hard to differentiate how someone had died, so he had gotten away with it for a long time.

'This was that guy's cover. Kate had no idea how bad this opiate crisis had become. Opiate deaths were at an all time high across the board, and everyone was looking the other way. Kate had to stop and take it all in. That look on that guy's face was so hard to read because she wasn't enlightened. She wasn't in on the misdirection. He had been caught. She caught him. Everything she knew, and had been taught about people, had been challenged in that moment. She knew deep down the public could care less about these people, but that's why she liked the job so much. She liked reminding people in the city that as they fought for all the assets and prestige, they were making peoples' lives worse. She liked the feeling of self-righteousness that came over her when she looked down on the privileged. She felt she was released from her own guilt, but this was different.

This was the accumulation of all that greed and ignorance. Society had created this guy, hiding in plain sight, taking advantage of the whole thing. He was the personification of indifference. How many times had he done this? Probably lots. This was worse than she thought. How long had this guy been doing this? The way he was right in the middle of the scene reminded her of Ted Bundy, and how he used to wear a cast so drivers would feel sorry for him and then pick him up. He would murder them after. He, like so many other serial killers, loved to help the police. The police would canvass the crowd around murder scenes just because of that. They would collect license plate numbers from all the cars that drove by.

This was perfect for this man who used a cane but obviously didn't need it. Kate remembers the story told to her by security after was that he fled the scene before anyone could catch him. He just banged on the door to alert staff with one hand and took off. Kate bet that if she hadn't found the girl, or even heard the death rattle, that guy would have just watched her gasp her last breath and then walked away. This guy, who was so involved in the first overdose just disappears after. Kurt said that the guy was over there all day and he wasn't even using drugs. This guy was the ultimate predator. Disguised by his street persona and hidden behind his disability, he preyed on the weakest. Evil hiding in plain sight.

13

KATE WENT BACK TO WORK WITH AN ANXIOUS IMPULSE TO GET THE names of the people involved, but how? The guy was gone and all she had was a first name 'Dax'. She didn't even know the name of the girl she had saved. She had never talked to her or even noticed her before this. Kate felt ashamed for not noticing her before. When Kate walked into the site office, she overheard a conversation about her last day. One of the staff said, "I wish I would have known about that guy. I wouldn't have let him in to use the bathroom" she said in shame.

Kate was beginning to realize that she wasn't the only one reeling from the trauma of this episode. She looked over the site staff and could see it written all over them. Kate could tell right away that she was being treated differently by the staff. She received warmer smiles and more help for things that she didn't ask for. Kate was relieved because she was dreading coming back to work. She thought she would be in trouble somehow, but it seemed to bring her and the staff who ran the site closer together.

Kate started to inquire about the woman she saved right away. "Maya hasn't left her room since the incident" was all Kate could find out. Kate went about the business of opening up the site after that with a feeling of relief mixed with a gnawing anxiety to find out the man's name. Kate spent the morning retelling the tale over and over again, to every support staff who asked and even to some who didn't. She was gaining confidence in her actions with every person she told. After Kate had told a half a dozen people, she went outside to get some air.

As Kate surveyed the scene, the Maya girl came out and walked right past her. Kate always found it awkward to see someone you had saved after the fact. It was like seeing a ghost. Maya was a little taller than most, with chin-length chestnut hair and pale, white skin. She was in her early forties, and her hands shook as she smoked her cigarette. Kate was afraid to approach her, what if I embarrass her? Or scare her away, Kate thought as she took in the sight of Maya, and with it, all the possibilities that could transpire from the encounter. Before Kate could finish her thought, Maya walked back inside the doors of the facility. Kate was relieved that she didn't talk to her, mostly out of fear. Kate had no idea what she would feel when she saw her again. Now she had. Now it was on to finding out her last name. Kate picked up her last name from the staff later that afternoon.

The day wore on, like they always do once a person settles in. The customers came and went from Kate's station with a regularity she had come to expect from the population. The customers used as much as they could stand it seemed, if they felt comfortable with you, they would nod right off and sleep, in front of you, sitting up in the chair. Kate understood the difference between sleeping and overdosing, which she would regularly have to explain to anyone who saw the clients in that fashion. Kate would reassure anyone who walked by and looked that "this is the desired effect. because if it was anything Kate knew, this generation wasn't interested in tripping out or community like in the 70's. All these people wanted was to check out, if only for a while.

For others, Kate wasn't so sure, sometimes after Kate would Narcan someone, she would watch them go back to where they were on the street curb and wonder if she had made a mistake. Kate wasn't always sure that these people always wanted to live. Kate understood that it wasn't her place to decide life or death, but she still wondered if the people would be better off dead sometimes. Sometimes a family member would come around looking for a client, and Kate would explain to them that she hadn't seen them and that she couldn't tell them even if she did. Kate would be asked if there was assisted suicide for drug addicts, to which she would reply, "if they want to commit suicide, don't tell them to come here; we don't let people die here. We've never had a death here at the safe injection site."

14

IT WAS AROUND 2:00 P.M. WHEN KATE FINALLY GOT UP THE NERVE TO approach Maya. "Hi," Kate said as Maya walked by her. Maya turned to her and said, "Hi" she obviously didn't remember Kate or at least Kate couldn't tell if she did. Kate went back and sat inside her site. She thought about her last shift and how things had happened so fast, but now as she looked around and watched the people bustle in and out; it felt like nothing had happened at all. This was something that Kate always marveled at about her job. No matter what happened, time would move on and the people would just roll with it.

Kate couldn't tell, but she had changed. In the months she had worked at the other facility and now here, she had gained experience and courage. She was no longer the scared girlfriend of a tragic figure. She was fighting back. She could feel the warmth of *his* hands coming back to her.

Kate's thoughts were interrupted by a client rolling into her space with a secret to tell. Dax's name was Dennis Ericson, and Kate could never tell anyone how she came upon the information. She wrote down the name she knew and put them in her pocket. She definitely wasn't calling the police again, not after that experience. Kate never liked police in the first place. It always seemed like they had something better to do, and they feigned concern when they listened to you like a parent who didn't believe you. She would wait for an opportunity, she decided.

At 4:00 p.m. when the security did their shift change, one of them walked up to Kate and told her, "That guy with the cane has been coming here at night. We've had to chase him off the property." Kate looked around the perimeter and felt an eerie feeling come over her. He wasn't hiding; he wasn't even running. He was waiting somewhere out there beyond the pale.

15

DAX MOVED AROUND IN THE NIGHT SEAMLESSLY. HE KNEW NOBODY WHO was looking for him would find him. He needed that pipe back. He needed the souls back where they belonged. As he pinned himself forward with his cane, he saw the Arena towering above the houses around Bay Street. He stopped at the 7-Eleven to get some smokes and see if anyone was around. Dax knew one thing about his look: He was invisible to all who moved around him. It had always been that way. He sometimes wore hard black lenses in his glasses and a black hat with his hair coming down the sides. But now since the incident, he had completely cut off his hair and was wearing a bright green cap with vanishing frames in his glasses. He knew that not all the security guards knew who he was, and it was only a matter of time before there would be new ones and he could get up close again. He lit a cigarette and caned his way down to the Crystal Pool and waited.

'That stupid bitch would be off at nine and as she walks away, I'll cozy up nice and close to the parking lot and wait' he thought.

Kate said goodbye to the staff at the facility as she packed up her stuff and went out the doors. It was a nice night out, and as the sun disappeared on the horizon, it left a crimson blue, cascade across the sky. It had been a great day for Kate. She had gotten the names, which at the beginning of the day had seemed like an impossible task. She was proud of herself. As she walked past the police station, she surveyed the cars parked outside. She crossed the road and made for a path between the church's buildings across the street, making sure nobody was behind her, and especially, that nobody was waiting for her as she made her way home.

Dax sent some scouts over to the parking lot to look for Maya. She was to be told to come over and see him. She was nowhere to be found. Dax never mentioned the pipe, but he did mention that she had something of his. Dax made sure that he told everyone he saw that night and the days after that it was bad dope. He even went as far as finding an Executive new hire and showing him bad dope that he had doctored at home. He would get ahead of this. He would control the information in this group. He would buy loyalty with dope, and he would sell his version of the story. When he was asked about the incident directly, he would plead that it was bad dope. When accused by people, he would laugh and say that story was ridiculous. Slowly, day by day and night by night, this tale would die, and a dozen new ones would take its place. Like the story of the man in the East End of Vancouver who would dose girls up, rape them, and then Narcan them after. The atrocities that flooded this population were in constant flux, and Dax knew that it would only take him showing his face and pumping good dope consistently to make any doubt about him disappear. Before the night was out, Dax got his pipe back. One of his scouts paid a resident to steal the pipe from Maya's pod while she slept.

16

GLORIA WALKED THE HALLS OF THE ROYAL JUBILEE HOSPITAL LOOKING for room 321. She had been to the crime scene, she had seen the suspect, and now she was trying to get a statement from the victim. She looked through the door of 321 and saw the victim lying there in his bed, barely conscious. The victim had been on the wrong end of an argument about a girl, and the suspect had put a flare gun in his mouth and pulled the trigger. They had to re-arrest the suspect because the pandemic protocol had made it impossible to hold him. Gloria was adamant on getting this guy locked up, and she just needed a few words from the victim to do that successfully.

She looked over the body and at the burn marks on the victim's mouth and neck. The job had become less sensical the last few years. The other cops on her detail spoke of the desperate acts people were involved in with embarrassment. This drug had changed things. The stuff they were seeing when you coupled the drug crimes with the pandemic hysteria were without consciousness. The nights that followed the first lockout of the homeless from their supports saw a wave of purge-like stabbings and other assaults. Revenge assaults mostly for the never forgotten crimes against the population. Police informing and petty theft from each other was the motive for most assaults. Gloria was swamped with hospital visits to people who didn't see their attackers because they were asleep or nodding on heroin when it happened.

Gloria approached the bed of the victim in 321 and made her presence known. "Hello, David. This is the police." He stirred for a moment, but then his eyes rolled back in his head as he fell back into a deep sleep. "I'm going to leave my card here. You call me when you can," she said as she left the room.

17

KATE LAY IN BED RESTLESS. SHE TOSSED AND TURNED FOR HOURS, STARING intently at the cracked bathroom door where the light shone in. She had slept with the bathroom light on and the door slightly opened ever since she found him. Kate's boyfriend was an addict. She had problems with drugs in her life that was no doubt, but when she started to go to school and get her priorities in order, she stopped. He never did. It was in her final year when it happened. She woke to find her boyfriend, Manny, dead in their bed. He was just lying there like a statue. His intent blue eyes were transfixed on the ceiling, and his body was ice cold. She woke to his cold hand draped across her thigh.

She barely finished school after that. Then one day she was reading the newspaper, and a story about the emerging opiate crisis jumped out at her. Until that moment she didn't know she was in shock. In that moment she didn't know she was cloaked in denial, passing from one task to another. She came to work at the safe injection site right after that. She had been saving lives and absorbing the city's pain ever since. She stared into the light that beckoned from the door. Her eyes blinked once, and then twice as she floated off to sleep.

Kate wasn't heroic or even brave by nature. When she met Manny, she was just a sheltered suburban chick who was running from all the pressure her parents had foisted on her to be a doctor. Manny was so exciting, even though he didn't think so. He would get depressed for days – sometimes weeks – and then he would explode into these runs that would last forever. They would go everywhere together. He could turn a regular, mundane landscape into a wonderland. Kate would be smiling so much that when Manny kissed her, he would kiss her teeth by accident. She loved him so much. He was her first everything. First crime, first hit, and even her first real orgasm. She thought she was having them before, but when it came to him, she shook every time he came near her. To be in the presence of that kind of captivation was a drug. She was hooked, and she would do anything he said. Kate lived through him, there was no doubt. She felt stronger with him by her side, and she would follow him down into his depression as well.

When he went down, she went down, and then she would explode out of the pocket with him into all sorts of capers. The man was a great con artist. He would always be working an angle on something. It got to the point where if he wasn't working an angle, she got suspicious. How Kate figured it was, if he wasn't working an angle, he was working someone else. She would get terribly jealous and ask him all sorts of incriminating questions. He would deny them, and she would put on an act straight out of Shakespeare, screaming and yelling. He would take off and not come back for days, and she would agonize over his absence until he returned.

She would wrap her arms around him and never mention the fight. The next episode would start building upon the last from that moment. The two were caught in the cycle that envelops so many young couples. It was only when Kate started going back to school that she stopped living through him completely. He felt the shift of energy leave his side immediately. He would go deeper into depression, but she wouldn't follow. He would explode out into the world, but she no longer followed. He started to do drastic things like stealing her books or hiding her papers. She learned how to placate him enough to earn good grades under his gaze.

School has a great way of making one need support emotionally in the downtime and complete freedom in the execution. She found for a while that this was complementary. He would go down after a test, and she would follow him a bit. When he exploded out into the world during a break, it was divine. She felt like she was living two lives. All the studying had made her crave adventure in any form she could find. They were able to make things work…sometimes. But he always got heavily depressed at the end of the summer. She knew that. September was hard for him, she could tell. He would start getting erratic when the leaves started to fall. He knew he would have to be alone more. Kate assured him it was her last year and that they would go traveling after. He acted as if he couldn't hear her.

It was early October that she woke up to him dead beside her. She could never forgive herself. How could she not see it? How could she not control it? The questions burned deep inside her without her acknowledgement. The expression of her grief came out in her work. There wasn't a situation that she wouldn't throw herself headlong into. She was daring, she was heroic, and sometimes in the silence of the night she knew it wasn't her fault, but that didn't matter, because she would get up in the morning, and it would start all over again.

When you work on the edge of society like that, you see a lot of death. It becomes your reality. It's like working at the airport for the soon to be departed. You get used to it, and before long, you get hooked on it. Nobody is more honest. Nobody is more real than the people who are living on that edge. There is nothing to hide behind. No status... No trophies. One stands arms open to death and welcomes it. This level complemented Kate's self-actualization. She was rising to it and thriving in it. This was the only way she could forget about him. With every life saved and crisis diverted, she was gaining her power back. She had come there a scared and anxious person. She had become willing and able to face death and despair aiding in its transformation.

In transforming this situation, she had transformed herself. Her perspective had changed, and with it, her whole world. Kate would watch the public walking around in their ignorance and comfort, and she would pity them. She felt as though she was given the gift of sight in the land of the blind. She saw people out there spending money trying to show off and she respected the panhandler more. She saw people packed into patio bars laughing, checking their phones, updating, snapping, and rating everything, and she was embarrassed for them. She watched people collecting bottles outside on the street and admired their will to survive, despite their status. She needed the place more than it could ever need her. She understood that. It was a blessing. It was a curse. That's just what happened.

18

GLORIA STOOD OUTSIDE THE POLICE STATION, LOADING GEAR INTO HER car at the start of her shift. She was deciding whether or not to bring a vest or just leave it. It was so rare for her to see any action – or even be where people were alive. She mostly showed up late to the party, which was all right with her. She remembered those police barbecues she used to go to when she was a kid, where her dad's friends would compare bullet scars. She never looked forward to those stories, that seemed to be told a thousand times, of how close people came. She was always afraid, as they all are of dying. She, like everyone else, would run into a hail of bullets because it was their job, she just never thought about it. Scared is what you were on a shift, fear was the only thing that would keep you alive when the storm came.

Just then, Gloria's thoughts were interrupted by a voice across the parking lot. "Hey, are you a cop?" a woman said to her.

Gloria had to think about it for a second. Did she really want to talk to this person? "Yes," Gloria finally said.

"Here are the names of the people involved with the two overdoses last Friday," the woman said.

"What's this?" Gloria asked.

"This guy gave people dope he had made at home, and I think he was trying to kill them," the woman replied.

Gloria's shoulders went back and her back straightened to meet the comment. Gloria's training kicked in automatically. "And what is your name?" she asked.

"Kate," the woman answered.

Kate looked over the officer and instantly regretted giving her the names. 'Nothing is going to be done about this,' Kate thought.

"I will look into this," Gloria said as she watched Kate walk away. Just that moment, Gloria felt a rush come over her. "Hey, how do I reach you?" Gloria called out.

Kate turned. "You don't," was all she said.

Gloria got into her car and thought for a second. As she turned on her computer, which was mounted on the console, her thought process was hijacked by the sound of her phone. "Hello," Gloria answered.

"You need to come down to the Jubilee. Your vic just passed," the voice said.

Gloria put her other foot in the car and closed the door. 'What a way to die,' she thought. 'A flare gun …'

19

KATE NEVER TOLD ANYONE ABOUT MANNY AT WORK, SHE NEVER WANTED anyone's pity or sympathy. She saw other women play the victim, and it never led to respect. All it ever got them was that they were deemed ineffectual and treated like fine china, only to be used for special occasions for fear of damage. Kate never wanted to be the girl who lost her boyfriend to the opiate crisis. She never wanted to answer to the tragedy. When Manny died, she had no idea what fentanyl was, let alone that you could die from it. She never really knew what he was using and when; he was always high on something, unless he was depressed or asleep.

She would still see him though, when she walked down the street, she would see him in the crowd staring at her, and then he would turn. But by the time she caught up, he would turn his face to her and it would be someone else. She started to see clients from work also, she would see the faces of the people she had saved walking with different bodies in her upper-class neighborhood. She would imagine that this is what they would be doing if they weren't down on the floor twitching and moaning into oblivion, she would see them walking arm and arm with their significant other or walking a dog. Everywhere she went, Kate was surrounded by the faces of the displaced and soon to be dead. They were her dream. She would walk around on her days off far from her work and be surrounded by all her clients, they would be living the lives they would have lived if they had not been taken hostage by that carnage. This is how she healed herself, this was how she found the strength to go back again and again.

She saw all those people from the streets all around her in every neighborhood she went. Everyone is everyone, they just don't know it. She saw how much luck played a factor in people's lives. 'One turn on the trail' is an expression she thought of often. A person only made one mistake in a myriad of successes and ended up down there on the floor scratching at the surface of the earth wondering where it all came from. All it took was one mistake or one stroke of dumb luck to send you up or down the scales of lady fortune. Kate wondered what kind of luck she would have now that she gave those names to that cop. She wondered what, if anything, would come for her now.

20

THREE DAYS LATER, MAYA WAS FOUND SITTING ON A PARK BENCH, HUNCHED over as if she was asleep. She had overdosed sometime in the night, she was dead. Kate had been talking to her, trying to get a picture of whether Maya remembered anything about that day or the man she was sitting with, but Maya couldn't remember anything. Kate asked Maya if any cops had come to talk to her about the incident, but she said no.

Death has a way of putting a quiet spell over a facility and Maya's was surely that for Kate. Kate thought about the first time Maya ever talked to her. She came up and accepted a cigarette and then went straight into it. "Um, literally, I'm just thinking about my son. I was molested by my foster mother, and she took my son away. I hear that he is trying to contact me, but the bitch won't let him. I hope he is okay. I think about all the stuff they could be doing to him, and I can't think straight." Maya took a deep drag of her cigarette and looked left to right.

Kate realized in that moment why Dax had picked her. She was quiet and unassuming. She had little friends and if she did have one, it wasn't for long. She walked around quietly talking to herself, sometimes screaming at people that weren't there. Her body was thin and frail, and her bright white skin flashed from underneath her clothes when she walked around. Her distended stomach was prominent when she wasn't hiding it, and she changed clothes several times a day to change her appearance. He was picking the weak and ineffectual, Kate could see that from what she witnessed. The first guy to go down the day in question was a non-resident from Vancouver and the second was her. Dax had been over there all day. If he had been giving that poison to everyone, they would have had a dozen overdoses. He sat, he waited, and he chose carefully all while in full display of the police station.

There was, just three overdose deaths that week, but there was a striking resemblance to them all. They were all women, of a certain background and all found alone. Gloria was there for all of them, picking up the pieces, following up with families if they had one. She recognized the name of the first one, Maya. She ran a check on her, and the file was thick with misdemeanor crimes, delusional outbursts, and restraining orders against her by her son. Gloria read the report from the Arena where the two overdoses were responded to and found the report about a man fleeing the scene after Maya's overdose. She looked up the name Kate had given her and found the record of a man well known by police. He frequented Rock Bay mostly but was known to venture into different areas to sell dope or solicit prostitutes. He had been convicted of statutory rape twelve years ago and served time. He must have hidden that from the community somehow, but then again, a man can have many names. Gloria looked over the report and saw the name Kate, as an employee of the Executive, who responded to the second overdose by herself. The report says nothing else except the individual in question would return at night only to be told to leave by security guards.

His alias was 'Dax' in the background check. Gloria was well aware of the type of man he was. Most of these dealer types preyed on the prostitutes that frequented the streets of the city. This type of man would smoke the last couple drags of a woman's existence and then put her out like a cigarette butt. Gloria knew she wouldn't get anybody to talk, and there were other families to inform about their loved ones' death. Gloria stared blankly out the window of the station. She never got used to the number of overdose deaths she was reporting since the beginning of the pandemic. The deaths had clearly doubled in her city and everywhere else in the province too. It used to be 75-90 a month now it was 175-190 a month.

This stat seemed crazy to her. If you close down safe injection sites you could expect up to seven deaths a week but not this many. She had never witnessed such a consistent dramatic rise in deaths in her city. 'There were so many women, too,' thought Gloria. The last three, including Maya, were all women, all found alone. Gloria shook her head. 'Something was wrong here. What if the one at the Arena was on purpose?' she thought. 'What if a lot of these are deliberate?' She pondered. How could she know? Gloria turned off the lights at the office and went home. She wasn't sure about anything yet, but something didn't feel right in her bones.

21

DAX LAY ON HIS BED, CLUTCHING THE PIPE TO HIS CHEST. HE DREAMED OF the time when he would join his lost souls twisting and turning in Sheol. He closed his eyes and pictured it. To be released from this existence was all he wanted; he envied his victims. It wouldn't be long before his work would be done, and he could ride that yellow nightmare into the distance. He was captivated by their last breath, he longed for it, he fantasized about it. He could feel darkness follow him. He had that power. He would approach her with a smile and leave her a gasping peasant. With every death, he could feel his power increasing and the time when he would descend nearing. He dropped off to sleep. He didn't dream anymore; he just floated there in Sheol with his ladies…

22

KATE SAT IN HER CHAIR, INSIDE THE ARENA SITE AND STARED AT THE WALL. There wasn't much action inside due to the fact that people had places to sleep, so they tended to use there. They didn't need to stay inside the site all day, like over on Pandora. Pandora's site was different; people would have their head in the middle of the table in a booth all day. They would even overdose on purpose, it seemed, in order to stay inside longer. The people at the Arena were stabilizing now, so they used less. Kate even saw the worst trouble cases transformed by the experience of stabilization. She would see these people walking around meeting other needs she didn't know they had, like eating or shopping.

Kate racked her brain trying to figure this situation out. 'How come the police never questioned her? Now she's dead? He must have got to her over there,' Kate thought, Maya didn't even remember him. Kate's head was spinning.

Everyone else around Kate seemed to go on as if nothing had happened, but that was what they were all used to. People died around them constantly, but there was always a story and an explanation. The street had its heroes and its code. If you broke those, you suffered the consequences. People shuffled in and out of the Arena all evening until it got dark, it was then, that they all just seemed to congregate outside. Kate locked up after she swept and mopped. She had already put supplies out for people so, they wouldn't need them and not have them in the night.

Kate went outside and locked up the smoking cage and just as she snapped the lock shut, she saw something out of the corner of her eye. It was him, Dax limping with his cane coming towards the building.

The Opiate Murders

There were crowds of people all around the parking lot, but she fixated on him. He had on different glasses: he had cut his hair short and had a green bowler hat on, not a baseball cap, but it was him. Unmistakable. He sat down with some people who had congregated at some benches about thirty feet from the building. He was oblivious. He did not seem afraid or interested in his surroundings. He didn't notice or recognize Kate, now leaning against the wall in shock, staring at him. Kate couldn't believe what she saw. How could it be that this guy, with all that he had done, could be sitting beside a police station, disinterested in his surroundings? Kate went inside and dropped the keys off. She walked out the doors and past the groups in the parking lot. She made it through the churches and past Pandora. She disappeared into the night.

23

WHEN KATE WAS IN SCHOOL AND SHORTLY BEFORE MANNY DIED, HE HAD taken her to a party out in Langford. Langford was the kind of place where all the crime was committed, but only a third of it was reported. Langford you could say was run by special interest groups. One of those groups was infamous, and in one of those groups was a man Manny had introduced her to at a party. The Bikers are a special interest group in Langford, but they are represented by many people. Murdoch was one of those people. Murdoch had come to Manny's funeral. At the funeral he had given Kate his number and told her if she ever needed something not to hesitate to call. Kate wanted something done about Dax, but she didn't know how to ask. What was the protocol for such a thing? She called the number and left a message.

Three days later, she received a call from Murdoch telling her to meet him at the Station in Langford and to come alone. Kate was a little freaked out by it all. What was she going to say to this guy? She arrived early, sat by the window, and ordered a glass of water, ignoring the smirk the waitress gave her when she ordered it. She felt like she had been sitting there a long time when he walked in. He was about six-four and weighed at least two hundred and fifty pounds. Murdoch wore black jeans, a shirt with a leather vest and a baseball cap on backwards. His face was pierced in various places with a great, big beard connecting it all. He sat down across from her and the whole booth shifted.

"Hey," he said as he lifted his chin towards her.

"Hey" Kate said.

"What's up? How are you doing?" Murdoch said as he tried to make out what he was dealing with. He kept looking over Kate's shoulder,

The Opiate Murders

probably scanning the crowd, like a lion would, making his presence known.

Kate studied his face carefully. 'He must have a mother,' she thought. 'Maybe even a couple sisters.' She took a deep breath and just came out with it. She started talking fast and leaning forward. She explained the situation at the Arena. She explained calling the police and giving the names to the cop outside. She explained the death of Maya and the reappearance of Dax. When she was done, she caught herself. She was afraid, the way a person gets when they expose their position too fast without taking in their surroundings.

Murdoch took a deep breath and absorbed what she said. He told her to go home, and he would be in touch. He was so cold about it that Kate was afraid for her life all of a sudden. She didn't trust her surroundings, and his reaction was not what she had anticipated. She got up and left him sitting there. The people in the room watched her leave, it could have been that they didn't care, or that she didn't matter, she couldn't figure out which, all she knew was that she was never coming back.

24

KATE TOOK A JOB WORKING FOR ANOTHER NON-PROFIT ACROSS TOWN IN one of the newly acquired hotel properties for the homeless. She needed to get away from the Arena, and all it represented for her. She started working for a recovery-based, non-profit dealing with the day-to-day needs of recovering individuals. The only problem was that nobody wanted to recover, so she spent her time delivering breakfast in the morning to people and walking around the facility talking with her coworkers.

The biggest surprise was that all the people she used to work with on Pandora, now had rooms to live in, and they had completely changed in appearance and stature. She would open a door and a person who used to be sleeping on the sidewalk freezing was now sleeping in a king size bed in front of a 56' inch screen T.V. Sometimes the person would still be sleeping on the floor though; it would take some time for them to get used to this life. She didn't even recognize them most of the time, and apparently the other staff didn't either. The residents needed to be photographed a second time after they had moved in because their appearances had changed so much. They were smiling in the second pictures, and they had gained color and weight in their appearances. Kate walked around in what seemed like a dream. She was so happy to see what stabilizing these people had done in two months what years of harm reduction and recovery tactics had been failing at for years. These people were sleepy and happy. The halls were quiet and clean.

Kate had forgotten all about her visit to Langford when she received a message to meet at the Fifth Street Grill on Hillside. When Kate arrived early, Murdoch was already there. He motioned for her to come over and sit. Kate looked around at the empty tables and felt a reality that they all were facing, the pandemic was scaring everyone into staying home. She did enjoy the service though. Murdoch took a long drink of his beer and set it down gently. "The situation we spoke of is being handled," Murdoch said.

"That's great," Kate said filled with excitement that she couldn't hide.

"No, I don't think you understand," he said.

"What?" Kate asked perplexed, her hands started shaking.

"There's nothing to be done." Murdoch finished his beer and stood up to leave.

"I don't understand," Kate said shocked.

"You told me to look into it, and I did. Do you understand?" Murdoch pulled his vest forward with both of his hands and looked out into the street. "He's being protected."

"By who? You?" Kate was reeling and tears started to form in the corner of her eyes.

"Not by us," Murdoch said, as he walked out the door and left Kate there crying into her drink.

25

DAYS TURNED INTO WEEKS AS KATE PICKED UP THE PIECES OF HER NEWLY acquired grief. How could this creep have protection? If not, protection why would people look the other way? Kate knew that she was an idealist, but this was murder. Not everyone saw these people as human, but nobody deserves this kind of indifference. Kate often ran into the opinions of other people she would think of as upstanding citizens. They would say that the homeless drug addict had given up on themselves. They would say that they chose this life for themselves, and if they could only just stop everything would change for them. Kate could never really believe her ears when she heard it. She wondered if anybody thought for themselves anymore, or was it just a few who thought, and the rest just followed orders. How else could this guy just be going around killing people with no recourse or consequence.

On Kate's first day off, she went back to Pandora to drop off her card key and noticed that all the buildings beside the site had been torn down – a church, funeral home, and an old condo. There were fences all around the grass areas where the homeless had first lived at the beginning of the pandemic. They had since been displaced: some to hotels, but mostly to parks, and even to Centennial Square in the heart of the city. Kate marveled at the speed of the construction projects that seemed to be erecting a building on every street corner around Pandora. Even during a pandemic situation where people were afraid to leave the house, they were slamming these buildings up.

Kate dropped off her key and walked past a few people she had saved from overdosing out on the street. When she saw someone she had saved, it was always surreal. Often, they looked at Kate, not quite knowing how they knew her, but Kate could never forget. Kate wondered what she was saving them from as she watched them sit in the same spot on the same block that she had found them dying in the first place, probably destined to do it again and again.

26

GLORIA SAT IN HER CAR OUTSIDE THE HOSPITAL AND THOUGHT ABOUT the last three months. There was an increase in overdose deaths in the region, that was obvious, but the volume of deaths is what concerned her. It looked like there was at least a third more deaths than there should have been. Gloria had nearly seen every one of them with her own eyes. Typical as they were there was something missing, there had to be. She was responding to sometimes two deaths a day, if not three.

Sometimes it was obvious, like when the ambulance protocol made the first responders take twice as long to put on their gear, by the time the paramedics got to the person, they were dead. This situation was becoming more and more common as the pandemic protocols continued. There were all sorts of fatalities that could have been avoided if the pandemic protocols were suspended, but that wasn't what seemed to happen at all. Even with the number of cases below fifty in a city of four hundred thousand people, the protocols were blindly followed. People died needlessly every day.

Gloria had witnessed enough death in the last four months, and it was beginning to wear on her. The thought of death from the pandemic was plastered all around her on television and in the news, but it was deaths completely related to the shutdown of citywide safeguards that brought the most grief to the populace. Hospitals and doctors' offices were at zero capacity. No new patients for non-emergent issues. People were dying of cancer before they could be diagnosed.

Gloria's eyes flickered as she scrolled down the reports. 'This would be a great time to kill,' she thought. 'Everything is shut down. Nobody is watching.' She started to think of the women she found and where she

The Opiate Murders

found them. Whenever Gloria found someone who had overdosed, she tried to imagine where the nearest Narcan was. Gloria would estimate it in kilometers. For the last three overdose deaths, the nearest Narcan kit was within five hundred meters, only half a kilometer. These ones always bothered her the most. To find someone that close to a Narcan kit was tragic. When you find someone dead you want to understand that there was no chance. Gloria could sleep well after finding someone dead if they had no chance of being saved, but this was different. These girls were in reach.

There was no sign of intravenous use with any of these recent deaths, they had all smoked. Gloria started to go back as far as she could in the database, looking at overdose deaths by women where they were found alone without signs of intravenous equipment. As she scrolled down the reports, she noticed a pattern emerge. The women who were found alone, had no signs of intravenous use but also were not found with the torch in their hand. It was a name that started back when the opiate crisis had begun, the torch was the pipe used to smoke down with, it would usually be clutched in the hand of the deceased. To the police and all those present, it was like a smoking gun.

The torch is dismissed a lot of the time because they were under the impression that the deceased was not alone. Common enough, is that the deceased started going down and the person with them just leaves because they don't want to deal with the situation. It is very common for the person to go down and not remember anything after. Information about this certain event is prevalent enough here in the reports. A lot of the time they get anonymous calls to 911 instead of someone staying with the person. The only problem Gloria could see is that nobody called the ambulance after these three women died. They were found without the torch, no witnesses and within five hundred meters of a Narcan kit. In a time when the paramedics were taking an extra fifteen minutes to respond to a call because of pandemic protocols, these women didn't have a chance. If Gloria was going to consider this angle, she would need to talk to some people in Narcotics about this Dax character. She had to be sure.

27

KATE LAY IN HER BED FOR DAYS WATCHING NETFLIX. SHE WANTED A DIStraction so bad she would watch anything. She watched *The Twilight Saga: New Moon*. She even started watching a show called *Connected*. She watched episode after episode connecting various themes in society. She watched how human feces was connected to fish and how the fish navigated their lives after coming into contact with heavily medicated excrement. They were unafraid of things they should have been afraid of because of antidepressants, and in the wild where there are predators everywhere, that wasn't good. She watched how a dust storm from a dried-up, salt lake in Africa provided the food for the Atlantic Ocean's fauna, and even eventually filled the missing link for the Brazilian rainforest's protein deficiency. It was all connected. That dust storm that started in Africa even poked holes in category four hurricanes, making them less potent once they hit the shore.

Kate thought of the memorials up and down Pandora for the opiate crisis. She thought of the plans the city had of moving all the homeless into L street miles away from Pandora. She thought of all the unaffordable housing going up around her. The most shocking thing to her was that the rent for apartments had nearly doubled in the last ten years. Now people were paying $1,600 to $2,000 a month for a one bedroom. There was no way anyone could afford these apartments, it was insane. Ever since the beginning of the pandemic, where the homeless people were being pushed into other neighborhoods, the crime and debris would follow. The newspaper was full of reports of increasing crime in their neighborhoods, along with public defecation because the homeless weren't allowed to use public bathrooms due to pandemic protocol. It was all exacerbated by needles being found where they never were before.

Kate started to think of the show *Connected*. Only this time she put the buildings going up as the catalyst. The city had plans for Pandora; that was no secret. They built Rock Bay landing to absorb the populace that would be systematically pushed that way, but it wasn't enough. This pandemic was the perfect opportunity to get rid of this population on Pandora for good. All the motives were as plain as day to her, and all the effects were too. Increased crime, excrement and needles could all be attributed to the homeless migration. The new buildings and the rent from the new citizens from other provinces coming to retire was the motive.

Kate felt sick to her stomach. Getting rid of as many as possible during the pandemic was the answer to shutting down essential services like safe injection sites and extending paramedic protocols when there was no tangible evidence to the contrary. All these things led to one very brutal reality for Kate as she stared at the bathroom light, off in the distance. Dax was necessary to the whole equilibrium of the structure. Nobody told him to do what he was doing, but nobody stopped him either. In fact, the city structure and goals allowed him to operate with impunity because, one way or another, he was doing what the city was trying to do, just faster. He operated within a niche that was prepared for him. It was open for manipulation. Kate sat up in her bed and gasped from the realization. She began to pace around her apartment. In order for this plan to work, the city would need one third of homeless people in hotels or low-income housing. This was how the governing body worked: It always gave you two thirds less than you needed. That's why welfare and the minimum wage were so low. They represented the exact opposite of what they implied: poverty management not welfare.

In order for the plan to work, the powers that be needed a lot of people to either leave the block or die. Not responding to the pleas from the block for the first month and a half of the crisis would provide the shock and awe needed for that. Many bodies were pulled from those tents in the early days. The fences, camps, and constant running off of groups on the block due to pandemic protocols took care of the rest. The final piece came to her from without. With the borders being shut down, heroin was scarce. Everyone thought the prices were going to skyrocket and that they would run out, but within a week, the prices had dropped and the product was so potent that an overdose advisory had to be put into effect. The month of April saw a 100% increase in overdoses across the province, and it continued every month after.

She sat down and marveled at the simplicity of greed. This mayor was pro-development, and she had blindly ignored the early months on Pandora – not because she was ignorant but because she was greedy. The proof was right there for anybody to see, except that nobody was there to see it because they were too afraid to come out of their houses or furious with people who weren't wearing masks. The distractions were multi-faceted, but they all pointed inwards. Did you wash your hands today? This hour? Am I too close to this person? Pan was the mythological figure from which the word "panic" was derived. Pan didn't represent disease; he represented fear. The real epidemic was fear. Kate saw that now. When people are afraid, they will give you everything just to feel safe.

28

GLORIA PULLED UP TO AN OLD, ABANDONED POST BESIDE THE NAVY BASE. She remembers it well from her earlier days on the force. Lieutenant Mike Spencer was there to meet her. Gloria had spent almost two years working out of this detail back in the 90s. She learned a lot, but wished she could forget most of it. She felt as though she was hung over for a year straight.

"Hey, Gloria. What brings you down to this part of town?"

"Hi Mike," Gloria said shaking his hand thoroughly.

"We miss you around here," Mike said as he looked at her cruiser.

Mike Spencer was a career Narcotics agent, who had started in Afghanistan in the army. Not post 9/11 – before that when they were fighting the Russians off. Mike had seen and done things that the department could only be proud of fifty years later kind of thing. Necessary, but definitely not on the level. Gloria looked him up and down as they chatted about the weather and the pandemic. He looked older, but only because all his clothes were from another time. She bet if he shaved, he could pass for forty. He even had a *Miami Vice* mustache. This man was from another era all together. Gloria shook her head when she thought about all the shit that this detail had been blamed for and how none of it ever stuck.

"Can I ask you something?" Gloria said, cutting through the small talk.

He raised his chin up. "What's up?" he asked.

"Have you ever heard of this guy?" Gloria said as she laid down a missing person's report she had drawn up and plastered on the internet in hopes of someone spotting him. Police use this as a tactic to catch criminals. They feign community concern over the whereabouts of set person in hopes of catching them.

"What did he do?" Mike says as he spat off into the distance.

"He might be connected to a string of overdose deaths," Gloria said officially.

Mike cut right through that. "What, like bad dope?" he asked.

"More like he made it at home and uses it on prostitutes kinda thing," Gloria returned.

"Why do you care about this?" Mike asked, lighting a smoke and exhaling just above her head.

Gloria knew Mike Spencer's take on the world too well. To Mike, life was a zero-sum game. If we lost a man, they win. If they lost a man, we win. There wasn't a lot of color; it was either black or white.

"I care because this happened right beside the police station, right under our nose, in plain view." Gloria had her back up. She needed this to settle in hard on him. She needed to rouse his sense of patriotic duty, because if she knew anything, this man did not care about hookers and junkies. However, this man would kill everyone in a six-block radius to protect a symbol.

"This guy is a bottom-feeding scumbag; he's a garbage man," Mike said, putting his finger in the middle of the face on the picture.

"So, you know him?" Gloria asked as her eyes widened.

"I know of him and dozens of guys just like him," Mike said, taking a long drag off his smoke.

"How do you know him?" Gloria asked quickly so she wouldn't lose momentum.

"It's not like I date the scumbag, Glory. I just know of him. He's a garbage man. Works out of Rock Bay. He's done time for statutory rape. An old friend of mine used him as a CI when we busted Fairheed." Gloria remembered that name: Fairheed was a human trafficker they had caught with a bunch of refugees a couple years back. They were being shipped somewhere, but they had never found out where.

"He's a CI?" Gloria asked gathering her faculties.

"More or less. Everybody is a CI, Gloria. You gotta know that," Mike said, looking at her out of the corner of his eye. Mike Spencer's detail

The Opiate Murders

had been accused a number of times of police brutality. The witnesses either changed their stories or disappeared all together.

"What do you think about this guy then?" Gloria just had to level with him; even though she knew the answer would be bad, she needed to hear it.

"This guy is just taking out the garbage, Gloria. Junkies and prostitutes are all on their way out anyway. It's only a matter of time. I don't know why you care anyhow," Mike stated, standing up straight and looking down at her. "I don't make them what they are. I just mop them up, hey girl?" Mike patted Gloria on the back as if to say farewell.

Gloria took a deep breath and said what she had come to say. "Do you ever wonder what side we are on?" Gloria said.

"Ours," Mike said coldly. "Say hi to your dad for me now and tell him it's been too long." Mike Spencer went inside his detail after that and didn't look back.

Gloria was surprised she had gotten that out of him. She knew what it was now. If there is a lion in the jungle, there are also hyenas. Dax was just that. Why he was operating with impunity right in front of the police station was something Gloria was going to find out. She knew what she just said to Spencer outside his detail would not be forgotten. He would go after this.

29

KATE RECEIVED A MESSAGE FROM MURDOCH TO MEET HER AT THETIS LAKE around 6:00 p.m. on Tuesday night. She came reluctantly. As she walked through the trail towards the lake from the parking lot, she thought, 'What if he's going to kill me?' But then she dismissed the thought as she said hello to couples and little kids walking with their swimming floaties and dogs. When she got out into the clearing, she felt the breeze hit her face. It was warm and dry from the sand with a hint of cold from the water. She remembered all the fun she used to have here when she was younger.

It's not like he was trying to stand out, but the dude just did. Off to the far right, along the water, she could see Murdoch sitting on a bench. He still had his hat on, but he had no shirt on, which at first looked like one because of all his tattoos. As she walked closer, she could see he had a bulldog with him asleep under the bench.

"Who's your friend?" Kate asked, looking into the eyes of a very tired dog.

"His name is Guillermo," Murdoch said softly. "He is more of an inside, nighttime dog," he said with a laugh. Kate felt more at ease and wondered why she was seeing him like this.

"I brought you here to tell you something," Murdoch said looking out at the lake. His green eyes lit up as if to meet the light that shimmered off the water. "Do you remember back in March when everyone was running out of dope?" he asked as he sat up and grinded his jaw shut.

"Ya, they thought they were going to run out in the East End of Vancouver and have riots," Kate said, recalling the pandemonium of the clients.

The Opiate Murders

"We were out completely, and our suppliers were shut out because of the borders being closed. We thought we were going to have to start knocking off pharmacies when we got a call. It was an old friend of ours offering us twice the potency at half the price," Murdoch said, looking around to make sure nobody was listening. "They only had one request that came with the supply." Murdoch said.

"What was that?" Kate asked.

"That we leave Pandora alone. No muscle. Just supply and look the other way," Murdoch said, lighting a joint.

"Are you fucking serious? You guys are the reason for the dope advisory?" Kate accused.

"Hey, since when has cheap dope with twice the potency been a problem?" Murdoch said looking at her sideways.

"True," Kate said, realizing the world she operated in.

"I never thought of why they didn't want us down there doing anything until you came around asking questions. I like you, so I just want to say this to you: Stay out of this," Murdoch stated ashing out his joint on the bench.

Kate took a deep breath, and then she turned to Murdoch and hugged him – not because she liked him and not because of what he had said, but because for the first time since this all began she didn't feel like she was alone in this. She felt validated. Murdoch absorbed the hug and put his big hand on the back of her head and patted it a few times. Just then Guillermo woke up and sneezed under the bench.

"Someone is up," Murdoch said. Kate laughed, and they both just sat there together. "Can you tell me why you are doing this, Kate? I mean, haven't you had enough pain?" Murdoch asked, obviously seeing the parallel between these overdoses and Manny's death.

"Every time I save one, I feel closer to him, like I can turn back time," Kate said as a light flashed in her bluish green eyes.

"It's not your fault, Kate. I don't know if anybody ever told you that," Murdoch said, rubbing her shoulder. She didn't know why she did it, but she leaned in far enough for him to kiss her. She soaked up his words and sank in for more. She wanted to feel safe for one moment. The exchange had left her shaking. She followed him to his car and then to his house. She left before she could wake them – both him and Guillermo sleeping in his bed.

Kate remembered the early days of the pandemic, when every moment it seemed there was a new story of impending doom. People would come into the unit at 6:00 a.m. just to gather their faculties from the night before. They would say, "That was wild last night!" All the old beefs and rivalries were being settled. Anyone who couldn't defend themselves was fair game. Kate and her staff had spent two days looking after a guy who had been hit in the head with a baseball bat. His jaw was smashed and his teeth cracked. The blood covered the floor. The guy who did it had been released from prison days before the assault, only to be let go again immediately after the assault. It was a time of virtual lawlessness.

The overdoses started to spike with the introduction of the new dope. Pure fentanyl at a discount leveled the field. The ambulances were running non-stop. Kate marveled at how this situation was exacerbated by the powers that be. They wanted the purge. They wanted the sweeping migration. They engineered disaster capitalism. Kate thought back on how Hurricane Katrina had changed the topography of New Orleans, and while the migration took place, the investors changed the zoning for the territory. When the people who owned the land came back, they were told that it didn't exist. There were going to be hotels there now. The same happened to the fishing villages where the tsunami hit in Malaysia. The Aboriginals' rights to the land were circumvented after the tsunami. There was going to be hotels there now too. Pandora was host to many Aboriginals, and after this disaster, their land was going to be taken away again. This time for condominiums and loft spaces.

30

KATE WENT BACK TO WORK IN A DAZE. SHE WAS USED TO THE ROUTINE now, but she really started to miss the action on Pandora. On the block, she had been afraid someone was going to die every minute. At first, she had dreaded going to work, but then after a while she got used to it. By the time she left, she was starting to crave the excitement. Besides the overdose in the parking lot of the hotel she worked at, Kate had only been involved with one other one. With the second overdose, she didn't even have to use Narcan because they caught it early enough: stimulation and time won out over Narcan and a visit from the paramedics.

This was a skill she had learned at the safe injection site that seemed invaluable to her now, as she watched anyone even looking like they were going to overdose being shipped off to the hospital, only to be kicked out five minutes later. Other than that, all she did was walk around and try to get to know the people who lived there. The only problem with this scenario was that nobody wanted to talk to her about recovery. They all seemed too busy with other things, like the day to day of hanging outside, fixing bikes, going to work, or getting high.

Most of them slept late and wandered around sleepy eyed. Kate started to see how some employees who worked in recovery could get the idea that they were imposters, but it only took a few minutes for Kate to realize a truth she had always known, and nobody would admit. Harm reduction has better numbers and works better because you are actively participating in someone's life by giving them safe gear and keeping them alive. In recovery, you waited around for them to want to stop in just the way and time recovery wants them to. Abstinence without any guarantee of housing is one of its biggest setbacks.

Homelessness in general is riddled with people who probably wouldn't use at all, or at least not as much if they had a place to live. Kate took a deep breath as she ran down the list of reasons in her head why people didn't want to talk to them.

One Saturday morning, Kate was standing outside the hotel when she struck up a conversation with Max. Max was a regular side user (crystal meth), and he would come and show the staff his pictures that he colored. He had a talent, and they all admired them. On that particular morning, they got around to talking about recovery, and he admitted that he had once had five years clean. He looked down at the ground and ran off a rendition of events that changed Kate forever. He explained to her that when he got to five years, he met a girl who was clean in the program, and they got married and had a baby.

He was working as a roofer. He got his cheque one Friday, and the fear and pressure of being a father and having to be a husband was so great that he went and picked up a ball of side and started using again. To make matters worse, he went home to his wife and got her using again. Sweat poured down his face as he recalled the tale. He explained that they were now divorced, and she had a no-contact order against him. He said he wouldn't ever consider getting clean again out of fear. The sheer embarrassment and shame he felt from relapsing was enough for him to lock that door forever.

Kate sat there stunned by the remark. Suddenly, she felt the intrusion of her presence there. She wasn't just reminding people that recovery is available, like she told herself. She was actively re-traumatizing the ones who had fallen short, which she suddenly and humbly realized was everyone there. The reality was that everyone at the hotel had heard of recovery, and most had tried it a number of times. You couldn't be homeless and not have tried it. Homeless was all you could ever be before without quitting completely. There was no housing-first paradigm.

Kate realized that her presence there was doing more harm than good. Even if by chance someone wanted to go to a meeting, they were all closed down because of the pandemic. The same was true about the detox and treatment facilities. They all took at least three months to get into, if you even got into the detox at all. It takes a lot more than just

The Opiate Murders

detox. She couldn't even look people in the eye when she talked about detox because she would purposely leave out the fact that you cannot smoke at the detox. She didn't mean inside either – not at all, not even outside. You also couldn't have coffee, sugar, or any other stimulant. No wonder success rates sat around 3% even with a five billion dollar budget in recovery. Kate knew it, and with all the uncertainty surrounding where or if you can go anywhere else after detox, she started to see why people didn't bother.

Kate also filled out a housing application for a man named Mikey, that she kept seeing sleeping outside of all the hotels she worked at. She checked on his previous applications, he said he had several. There was none. She got him one, and it was active. She was excited, but he wasn't. She realized later when she had a friend run his name that it had been taken down again. She was disillusioned by it.

Kate resigned from the job and took three weeks off. She was hoping that being busy would help her forget how vulnerable she had been that night with Murdoch. She hated showing that part of herself to anyone, but after all, she was a woman and she appreciated him for being there for her. She thought about that night shamefully when nobody was watching. She kept the memories safe inside herself and visited them often. She also spent significant amounts of time looking at pictures of bulldogs. She had grown very fond of them in the last little while. The suffering of waiting for a text from him outweighed the sheer terror of texting and waiting for a reply, so she chose the former. She surrounded herself with fiction books and pillows. She occasionally let pay-per-view wash over her as she waited for her next adventure. She often wondered what would come for her but couldn't formulate the will to go after anything. She waited for the volition to return, but it seemed to escape her constantly. She was without a why, and as anybody knows, a why can sustain any, how.

31

HER WHY CAME IN THE FORM OF "RENT", WHICH SHE GLADLY LEFT HER bed to go out and pursue. She would return to the place it all started: working for the Executive at the Arena. She was excited to see that people there were being moved off to permanent housing. She also ignored the fact that some also moved over to the Crystal Pool baseball fields across the street to live. She could see the containers they gave people at Topaz Park outside the tents around Crystal Pool. These people were just being moved around by the city.

She was back in the harm reduction game, and she felt revived. Previously, she had it in her mind that recovery was more rewarding. It does pay a little bit better, and it seemed like the intentions were good, but she knew now that it was like selling tickets to a carnival that never comes. She was elated to see her old regulars and hear their concerns. Not everybody knew where they were going, which made them jealous of the ones who did. There was lots of added tension, but to Kate's surprise, most of the people there had gotten used to the place. It was astonishing the conditions people could get used to: no walls, no locks, and everybody getting their stuff stolen 24/7. How they did it she had no idea.

That is what being at this level had taught her the most. Gratitude. For her situation, her little apartment, her life. 'We have no idea how good we have it, because it's just another day for us in paradise,' she thought. These people treasured every meal, blanket, item they had. To have a new pair of shoes was a luxury. A shower was divine. She was glad to be back, standing on the edge, where life made sense for her. Harm reduction would be her bread and butter while she waited for greater things.

32

KATE LOCKED UP THE SMOKING CAGE OUTSIDE THE ARENA PROMPTLY AT 9:00 p.m. She had made her intentions known for the past thirty minutes, so there would not be any confusion. There were only a few stragglers, but they made their way out of the tent as soon as they could. Kate dropped the key off with the site office and started making her way across the parking lot, past the police station, and across the road. She slipped between the church buildings into a dark parking lot, but something didn't feel right to her.

Kate looked to each side, scanning behind her with her peripherals but saw nothing. She took another step and then she heard a step. She stopped. It stopped. All the hairs on the back of her neck stood up to meet the fright that ensued. She turned around and looked back between the buildings where she could see a shadow appearing – that was all she remembered. Something hit her hard across the back of the head and kept hitting her until she was unconscious. She receded into the background of her life. She remembered her ninth birthday party she carried with her a red balloon. She was so proud of it. Somewhere along the way into the backyard, it slipped out of her hand. She tried her best to chase after it, but it went up faster than she could run. Eventually, it was so high that she couldn't get it back even if she could fly. All she could do was watch it go until it was gone.

When Kate opened her eyes, she was in a very bright room. There were flowers on a table to the right, and the window was covered by a partition. She ached all over. She could tell that her face was hurt because of how tight it was. She couldn't really lick her lips, but she tried. She was so hot she was sweating. She fell back asleep for what felt like days. When she woke again, a nurse was adjusting the machines on her left, and then she was asleep again. She could hear people talking about her in the background of her dreams, where she was either running or swimming. She couldn't really decide which it was; maybe it was both. She never did catch what she was chasing.

When she opened her eyes again it was the doctor she was looking at "Good afternoon, Kate. My name is Dr. Hanlan. How are you feeling today?" she said with an ounce of concern.

"Sore," Kate said as she listened to the sound echo out of her head.

"Do you remember what happened to you?" the doctor asked.

"No, it was so dark," Kate said sitting up.

"Well, you've sustained some injuries to your head, neck, and face. The blow you suffered didn't break anything, but you do have a concussion. You have been unconscious for three days. We are going to keep you for observation until we feel you are ready to go home. Do you have any questions for me?" she said briskly.

"No," Kate said. Looking around and spotting a plate of food, she grabbed at it and was helped by a nurse. "I'm starving," Kate said as she shoveled food into her mouth. It made the back of her head hurt, but she didn't care.

"That's good," said the doctor. "The police might be by later to take a statement," the doctor added as she left the room.

"Your mother is on a list to see you, but because of the pandemic, she will be the only one," the nurse said as she adjusted the pillows behind Kate.

"Okay," Kate said as she finished the food.

"My name is Millie, and I'll bring you another plate. You just rest up" and the nurse walked out.

Kate slid back down the pillows into a deep sleep. She didn't care about anything except that.

When Kate awoke, it was morning. She could tell because the blinds had been drawn, and she could smell coffee. She reached for the plate nearest to her when she saw Gloria sitting in the corner of the room on her phone.

"Hey," Kate said as she continued with her mission for sustenance. As she started to eat the breakfast left for her, she watched Gloria stand up and gather herself together. Gloria was tall and blonde. She was still beautiful, but not the way she used to be. Some would say she was tolerably beautiful. Kate looked at Gloria's cop shoes and took a sip of her coffee.

"This coffee is disgusting," Kate said as she winced and swallowed it.

"I bet," Gloria said as she opened up her note pad. "Do you remember me?" she asked.

"Ya, you're that cop from the parking lot," Kate said as she searched for something to put on her toast. 'Mmm, peanut butter,' she thought.

"Do you remember anything from the other night?" Gloria straightened the pen out between her fingers.

"No, it was dark, and I was hit from behind," Kate said, very awake all of a sudden.

"Anything else?" Gloria said with a sigh.

"I heard footsteps, and when I turned, I saw a shadow. That's when it went dark," Kate said.

"A shadow?" Gloria asked.

"Ya, between the buildings. I thought someone was coming up the alley," Kate said, taking another sip of the coffee.

Gloria knew that alley. You could see it from the front desk of the police station. "You never actually saw the person though?" Gloria pressed.

"No, but I was about to, I think," Kate said as she got really hot again and started sliding down the pillows. "Every time I eat, I fall asleep," Kate mumbled.

"It's okay. That's all I need for now. I left my number beside your phone if you think of anything else," Gloria said as she packed up her stuff.

"Wait," Kate said.

Gloria looked at her and smiled. "Yes?" she asked.

"What's your name?" Kate said with that last twinkle in her eye.

"Gloria," she whispered.

Kate fell asleep as Gloria rushed out of the room. She got into her car and logged into her computer. She searched the cameras from that night until she found it. She watched the feed and kept fast-forwarding until she saw Kate walk by and across the street. She didn't see anyone else. Kate disappeared into the buildings and then there was nothing. Gloria switched cameras to the front desk camera and sped through it. Then she saw it, and a huge smile came across her face. From the other direction, a man came down the street and turned down the alley. He limped. She focused the camera, and it was him. Dax. She couldn't believe it. He was the one walking up the alley. But who was the other? There was no security camera on the other side of the building.

33

WHEN KATE WOKE UP THE NEXT TIME, SHE SCROLLED THROUGH HER phone. Texts from all sorts of people were waiting, explaining that they weren't allowed in the hospital to see her. Lots of well wishes. Then she saw it. Murdoch said one thing: "I'm on it." A tear came to Kate's eye. She felt so alone that when she saw the text it became her, and she started to cry. This had been so hard, all of it.

Just then Kate's mom came in with a coffee, and Kate started to cry more. She laughed too. "I love you, Mom!" was all she could say as she wiped her eyes and then put one hand on the side of her head to meet the pain that followed.

"I'm so glad to see you awake, honey," her mom said as she hugged her and kissed her on the cheek.

"I'm so glad you are here!" Kate felt very dizzy and she slid back down the pillows and cried herself to sleep.

34

GLORIA DROVE AROUND IN HER CRUISER, THINKING AS SHE DROVE. SHE thought about the overdoses she had been seeing over the years and how some of them didn't feel right. She never liked losing the young people to this epidemic, but she wasn't entirely numb to the deaths of the older ones either. She drove past Crystal Pool and studied the shanty town that had been strung up over the past couple weeks by the homeless in tents. She felt empty. Not the kind of empty that comes with numbness, but the kind that comes when you are all prayed out. She had to do something. It was crushing her soul to watch this happening to her city.

She drove across the Bay Street Bridge and past the parks and train tracks that gated Esquimalt. She drove right up to Mike Spencer's post out there at the navy base and left the engine running. She tried the door. It was open, so she just let herself in. The rooms were typical with bulletin boards and desks —mostly lawn furniture. She saw a scooter in the corner, which seemed odd to her but then she turned around quick to meet a feeling that she got that she wasn't alone.

"Hey, what's up Glory?" Mike said as he put his hands on his hips beside his gun and badge and leaned back a bit on them, pushing them both forward.

She didn't have time for niceties. "Where is he?" she said in a low tone.

"Who?" Mike said looking off into the distance out the window.

"Your CI," Gloria said with anger bubbling in her stomach.

Mike's eyes seemed to dilate as he took a few steps forward. He looked at her for a minute and then exhaled. "I don't know. I thought you knew," he said scratching his head and acting aloof.

"Stop fucking around. I know you know where he is. You wouldn't be you, if you didn't," Gloria said with a confidence that reached past familiarity and deep into contempt.

"Now if I didn't know better, I'd think you were trying to say something to me without saying it," Mike said nonchalantly.

"I know you know where this guy is. I don't know why you are hiding him, but I'm going to find out," Gloria said.

"Now I'm starting to get the feeling that you have forgotten where you are and what you are," Mike said looking out the window. "You see out there? This is Federal property not City property. I'm God out here. So, take your tin badge and prop gun, and get the fuck out of here, right now, before I retire the both of them. You come around here talking that shit again, and that's just what I'll do," Mike said raising his voice just loud enough to register concern to Gloria that she was out there with no real proof or justification. She knew it though. She couldn't prove it, but she knew. This crooked, washed-up prick was covering for him. She just didn't know why. She drove away satisfied that there was more to this story and that she wasn't completely crazy.

35

GLORIA KNEW BY GOING OVER THERE SHE HAD JUST STEPPED ACROSS A line that most officers stay clear of. She had just broached a superior officer of another unit. A unit that deals in deception. She was reluctant to visit her father because of all the questions and insinuations she would have to hear from him about her divorce. Gloria had married a cop, and by the time she found out that was a mistake, her daughter was well on her way. She felt trapped by a blue cage that pervaded every angle and gasp of fresh air in her life. By the time her daughter Amanda was six, the relationship was over, and they divorced.

Her dad was on her ex-husband's side during the divorce. He was old school, and Gloria's mother had died a saint when she was young, so he never had the time or the reality that Gloria suffered in her marriage. Gloria felt betrayed, and they hadn't really talked since then. Amanda would go visit sometimes, and Amanda and her grandfather were the ones who attended the barbecues now. Gloria stayed out of it. She pulled into her dad's driveway contemplating what to do. Did she have a choice? She sat there for a few moments and thought back to what her mom would do.

Gloria never knew her mother, but she had pieced her together out of old stories her grandparents had told her and daytime TV. She knew her mother would stand up for what she believed in and would follow her hunches to the end. Gloria had built a grand archetype of her mother. It had even come in handy when she left her marriage and had to stand up to the force and the family. 'Mom would go in there and tell him what's what,' she thought to herself, as she got out of the car. She walked up the old driveway, passed the old doghouse, and came in through the basement. She could hear the sound of the game coming from upstairs as she ascended the steps to the living room.

"Oh my God, Gloria you scared me," Mel said holding heart. "Jesus Christ!" he yelled, which was as religious as he got.

Gloria took a deep breath while he caught his. She sat down next to him and told him everything she knew. She stared blankly at him when she was finished, and he stared at the TV.

"I wish you would have come here first, kid," he said in regret. "I always want you protected regardless of how things are between us" he said as he looked to a picture of Amanda over the fireplace next to Gloria's mom.

"What can we do?" Gloria said quickly so he didn't lose focus.

"I'll make some calls, and get in touch with you later. What time are you off shift?" he asked.

"Six," she said looking at her watch.

"I'll get back to you then, when I know more," he said watching Gloria get up and adjust her uniform.

"I'm glad you came here, kid," he said to her with a tear in his eye. She knew that he missed her, but right now there was nothing to be done. She left his house feeling a weight had been lifted. She had told somebody else what was happening. She drove back down to the precinct and parked her car, leaving it running idle while she checked the security tapes again.

There was no doubt that it was Dax, but he must have followed her there from over here she thought, so she checked the arena cameras. She spotted something. Over in the corner, next to the dairy plant, sat an unmarked police cruiser. She could tell one of their own instantly. She watched Kate leave the Arena, and then watched the car slowly creep down the road and around the block in the direction of the church on Quadra. Then it disappeared into a blind spot. They didn't have a camera over there. The witnesses who found Kate said they had found her there alone bleeding on the ground.

Who was in that cruiser? She checked the logs for her precinct. It wasn't theirs. She felt that pang in the bottom of her stomach again. She knew it was Spencer's doing. She had to sit back in her seat and take it all in. How many of these overdoses were murders? How long had this been going on? Years? Her head was spinning. She needed some time to sort this all out.

36

"YOU'RE GOING TO HAVE TO FIND A ROCK TO CRAWL BACK UNDER, AND I don't think Rock Bay is far enough," Mike Spencer said as he kicked the foot of the chair Dax was sitting on.

"Back to the East End?" Dax said in a whimsical tone. "I always knew I would end up there. Personally, things are just easier there. Nobody gives a fuck, not like here," Dax said spitting on the ground.

"I really don't give a fuck. You just can't stay around here. Pack up your scooter and let's get your shit out of here," Mike said as he went out to start the car.

"What about the girl?" Dax asked.

"She woke up," Mike said, climbing in the car.

"You'd think that you cops would be beyond reproach for that kind of thing," Dax said packing a bag.

"C'mon, we don't have all night," Mike yelled from the driver's seat. A moment passed between them before Mike said, "And make sure you send someone else over here."

37

KATE SCROLLED THROUGH HER PHONE, TRYING TO KEEP UP WITH THE messages coming in from her camp. 'A near death event really brings them out of the woodwork,' she thought. Just then, her mother came in with coffee. "Oh, thank God, you are here. I almost drank that putrid stuff from the kitchen," Kate said with heightened exuberance; she was feeling better. The doctor wouldn't object to saying she was well on her way to a speedy recovery.

Kate's mom had fussed over her hair since the incident because so much blood and debris were mixed into it. "Thank God, they hit you in the back of the head. It's easier to hide scars back there," her mom said.

"I'm not going on any dates any time soon," Kate returned.

"Not even with the bulldog man?" Kate's mother, Pammy, loved to tease Kate whenever she could. There were so little opportunities to do it nowadays because she had rarely seen her daughter since Manny's funeral. Kate hadn't cared much of what Pammy thought about her new job. Pammy had to find out from someone else. But now watching her daughter, she knew that Kate liked someone. Ever since she was a little girl, she would keep secrets from her mother but the distance between them always gave her away. Kate didn't know this, of course, but Pammy always knew.

Kate ignored the comment and kept scrolling while she sipped her coffee. Her screen saver had a bulldog puppy on it now. Pammy felt safe that her daughter was going to be okay, inside and out. This had been one hell of year for them all. She was glad they were spending so much time together; she just didn't like the circumstances or the hospital. She wondered if her daughter would want to move back in with her. She hoped so. She also hoped Kate would give up this crazy life. Only time would tell.

38

GLORIA RECEIVED A CALL FROM MEL THE NEXT MORNING INSTRUCTING her to go see an old friend of his from Spencer's detail, who took early retirement at the beginning of the pandemic. Gloria drove out to Sydney to meet Roger Paddick. He was on the force twenty years with a number of different outfits. He worked mostly in Narcotics, but he did some moonlighting in anti-terrorism and other agencies when needed. His retirement was a shock to most, but then again, you never really know how much pressure someone is under until they crack.

'Sometimes people just retire,' Gloria thought as she drove up to the house. She took a long look across the bay and imagined her own retirement. Seemed like a dream from where she was sitting. She took a deep breath and climbed out of the car. 'You can always tell when one of ours is retired,' she thought. Not a blade of grass was out of place on this guy's lawn. There wasn't a chore left for him, to get him out of the kitchen,' she thought. He must drive her nuts, Gloria thought as she peered in the window. She knocked officially on the door and heard a woman yell, "Roger get the door." The door opened and there he was very awake and ready to go. Gloria always admired older gentlemen. They were always all dressed up even with nowhere to go. Roger was no exception. 'At least he isn't wearing a tie,' she thought.

"Hi, Gloria. I'm an old friend of Mel's. I recognize you from Mel's pictures on the mantle," Roger said as he slicked back his recently wetted hair.

"Nice to meet you," Gloria said shaking his hand.

"Do you mind if we step outside? I don't want to disturb Marjorie," he said as he led Gloria to an even more manicured backyard. Gloria laughed to herself that he had only been retired three months, and this place looked like a wax museum with gnomes, turtles, the works. All complete with a ten-foot deer fence lined with mesh, just in case.

"I love your yard," Gloria said out of habit.

"We do love it," Roger said under his breath.

Gloria instantly felt the pressure this guy must have been under. 'I'm so glad I got divorced,' Gloria said to herself as she averted her eyes from his gaze.

"Well, like I told Mel on the phone, I don't know how much of what I have to say will help you," Roger said anxiously. "Do you want any coffee?" he interjected.

"No, I'm fine," Gloria returned. "Well, Roger anything you could do to help would be greatly appreciated, as you know." Gloria wanted to be reassuring, but it was hard because she had no idea what he was going to say.

"I worked with Mike Spencer's detail over at the base for the last three years." Roger looked off into the distance.

"Okay," Gloria said, coaching him on.

"Well, you know all this defunding the police stuff you have been hearing on the news in the States?" Roger said.

"Of course," Gloria said.

"Well, it started a long time before that. When the opiate crisis began, money started to be funneled away from us and into things like harm reduction workers and nurses and all that," Roger said.

"Okay," Gloria said vaguely grasping the idea.

"Well, it kind of split the department at the top. You know, Gloria, that the government barely gives us a third of the money we need to get the job done, and now they were going to divert funds away from the little money we were already getting. It made some of the top brass go crazy," Roger said.

"Okay, I don't really read those memos," Gloria said still at a loss.

Roger started with a deep breath and then just went into "the funding being diverted elsewhere was greatly resented by some because that meant there would be less cops, equipment, and hours to deal with a problem that we were already maxed out on. Those junkies out there would be chewing into our bank, essentially. So, what started to happen with some officers is they would start to turn a blind eye to anything, and anybody, connected to overdoses."

"Mike Spencer, you mean?" Gloria interjected to bring things home to a workable subject.

"Yes, Mike and the others were very pissed off about the diverting of funds," Roger repeated.

"Well, how do you mean, 'turn a blind eye'?" Gloria asked.

Roger leaned forward and said, "You know how they decriminalized dope in other countries like Portugal, for instance?"

"Yes," Gloria said.

"Well, let's just say that some people stopped investigating overdose deaths all together."

"What do you mean?" Gloria asked.

"If they were going to divert all the resources over to harm reduction, then the nurses and the harm reduction workers could figure it out," Roger said.

"But they would obviously report any wrong doing," Gloria said flippantly.

"Ya, but then that report would get buried under another report of an overdose death, which would be rendered outside of their jurisdiction. They declassified them. Why else would these deaths rack up so high so fast? It's not just fentanyl that is killing people. Think about the people letting it sell, and now think about cops diverting their responsibility over funding," Roger said looking off into the distance.

Gloria sat there for a minute and thought. "Is that why you retired?" Gloria asked.

"I knew as soon as the safe injection site got closed down that we were going to see a 100% increase in overdose deaths across the province. When the smoke clears, there are going to be a lot of questions asked about the numbers, and I didn't want to be involved. I wasn't going to spend the last years of my career making excuses for the union," Roger said with reverence.

"What does the union have to do with this?" Gloria asked.

"This is happening everywhere, and I mean who can blame them really? These junkies aren't people. They are animals and discarded waste to most people. It was easy for them to do this. Nobody cares," Roger said finally.

Gloria looked at him for a moment and then back at the table between them.

"I mean, it's a tragedy when we lose a young one, and you know, we investigate that. But I mean one of these prostitutes or lifers from Pandora. You know we just bag them and move on," Roger said with finality.

Did you know Mike was involved in some of these overdoses?" Gloria said finally.

"No, but aren't we all to some degree?" Roger said, wiping his forehead.

"I mean, you worked with him. How could you not see it directly?" Gloria accused.

"Listen, when the whole town is looking the other way, it's pretty easy," Roger answered. "And then again, I could ask you the same question," Roger said.

"What is that supposed to mean?" Gloria snapped.

"You went right to him, didn't you? You already knew, it just hadn't directly involved you. You are just like any of us. You count your overtime hours and the days to your retirement. The only difference between us and the shipyard is that they don't get to shoot anyone." Roger stood up one second before his wife's call came for him.

Gloria stood up and shook his hand. "I'll be in touch," she said, as she took the side gate out.

39

KATE LAY AWAKE IN THE MIDDLE OF THE NIGHT, GOING OVER AND OVER every detail she could remember. The sense of fear would make her feel as if her bones were tightening around her. Something wasn't right. 3:21 a.m. came and went as she swam through her conscious imaginings. What was she to do now? She couldn't go back to work, could she? What about all the people out there? She felt her need to help others exceeding her desire for self-preservation. She didn't know where those people ended, and she began. She was drowning in a sea of empathy, swimming as far as she could get away from her own reality through them. Her thoughts finally gave way to her dreams, and she floated away.

When she awoke, the doctor was standing over her and whispering with the nurse. Kate couldn't make out what they were saying, but she sensed urgency. She rubbed her eyes and was quickly hit with a few "good mornings" and a "how are ya feeling today"? The old hospital two-step.

"I'm alright, Kate said as she coughed into her elbow and sat up. She took a sip of water and looked around the room while she rubbed one eye completely red.

"We've been going over your chart and everything looks good. You should be able to go home within the next couple days," the doctor said.

"That's great," Kate said yawning into one arm.

"One last thing," the doctor said in a whisper.

Kate's stomach tensed all of a sudden. She didn't know why. "What?" Kate asked.

"We did and have been doing a lot of bloodwork here at the hospital. It seems that you are pregnant." The doctor handed Kate a brochure for Planned Parenthood and stepped back again.

Kate was lost for words. At first, she thought it was funny but didn't make any facial recognition because she was in shock too. There was a number of different thoughts and emotions that came up to meet the news – none of them she was necessarily fond of.

"Would you like to talk about options now or should we come back? I know this must be a surprise," the doctor said.

"Well, ya," Kate said with a laugh of pure astonishment as she watched them leave.

She was going home soon. That was the only part she was willing to think about. But slowly as the silence crept in on her and the door shut, she started to think of the only person it could be and how completely bad the timing on this was. She was lucky she was alive, let alone pregnant with that man's child. She tried to go back to being sleepy and lethargic, but her pupils were dilated. She waited for her mother to arrive, going over whether she should tell her or not.

'OMG, Kate. Don't say anything. What are you thinking?' was her last thought on it. She decided then and there to keep this one to herself until she figured out the next move. 'You have time,' was the still small voice she heard to soothe her panic. She was flushed with emotions. She scrolled through her phone to his text. 'I'm on it' she read, over and over again, as she thought to herself, 'You have no idea.'

40

GLORIA WOKE UP EARLY THAT MORNING AND WENT OVER HER CONVERSAtion with Roger. She thought about going over to see her dad, but all the old adages had returned, and she recoiled from the thought. 'No need to involve him any further,' she thought.

Gloria started thinking back over the years about all the cases that she had investigated. She thought about her procedures and how Roger described something she did religiously: She classified deaths the same way he explained them – from tragic to common. Nobody was looking for the people that Dax was preying on, least of all the police. That's exactly why he chose the women he picked. 'And who knows how many men,' she thought. Nobody even blinks when a man dies of an overdose.

There had to be witnesses if the scope for this was big, but if the method of murder was overdosing, it could be huge and totally untraceable. When she registered an overdose death, she was looking to rid herself of the paperwork and move on; that's how common the procedure was. She was exactly what Roger had described. She left it up to the paramedics and first responders. She had better things to do.

That was the weakness in the system that was being exploited and that is why Dax was sitting outside the police station poaching people. He knew that if he picked people on the fringe of the group, he would not be blamed or investigated because people who nobody cares about don't matter to the system. The system is designed to bag and tag the fringe population. If they were from out of town or had slipped to the bottom of the dominance hierarchy of the street, they were meat. The older, the better.

Gloria took a deep breath and wore the accusation like a cross to bear. If she was the problem, how was this ever going to end? She felt she cared about people more than the next officer, but if she was actively participating in this, then what could she do? She couldn't go to Internal Affairs about this. Her reports were exactly the same. She was part of this. All those people were classified as animals and discarded. It was systematic, and it made her sick, but at the same time, she felt helpless by it.

How could we stop an epidemic when we are willfully perpetuating it?' she asked herself. 'If we knew how to improve the situation, it would be improved. We have degraded to blaming the population for dying because we think they are seeking it. Its not like, this isn't a psychedelic trip they are seeking. Nobody is expanding consciousness here. They are checking out. You seek a psychedelic trip to expand your consciousness, you ingest opiates to escape from the pain of a cruel world. Gloria could never figure it out, but now she saw it for what it was, a last resort. Sometimes it was easier not to think about it. She had known many good police that burned out like a comet hitting the atmosphere chasing 'meaning' around.

Gloria decided to stick to what she could prove. She started scanning video footage going weeks back...

41

KATE LAY IN HER BED, COUNTING DOWN THE LAST HOURS BEFORE SHE WAS to go home. She had moved past shock and denial; she was now well into anger and depression. How could you be so stupid? It was only one night!' she thought. She hadn't even thought about having sex since Manny died. When she missed her period, she had just thought it was the drugs from the attack that had her off cycle. She just imagined it away.

The thought of having another abortion made her cringe. She lost all sense of feeling in her stomach when she thought about it. It felt like a cauldron of burning acid had opened in her abdomen. She didn't know if she was ready to go home.

Do you think they would let me transfer to the Eric Martin psychiatric unit?' She thought. 'I can't have a baby! She buried her head in the pillow and cried as hard and as ugly as she could before her mother came.

Maybe there's a way. She sometimes interrupted herself with a string of possibilities and scenarios that had no bearing in the real world. She would start with imagining away all negative circumstances then she would take away other constraints like money and time. Next, she would follow that up with disturbing the physics of it. She would imagine that she was a Mary Poppins-like figure with color cartoon animals that followed her around. She would fly from place to place and take care of children that she had, but never had to give birth to. She would be well sought after by families everywhere. She would sail in and fix problems, extol wisdom, and then be on her way…

What a life that would be.

Just then, her mother came through the door carrying flowers and a coffee. Kate couldn't stop a final tear rolling down her cheek. She secretly envied her mother, and all other mothers in the world in a way she never could before. They were such strong people. Fearless, it seemed, for appearing so ordinary. She received her flowers gracefully and took a sip of her coffee. She left the hospital that day not knowing what she was going to do, just like so many others in her predicament. She held onto her imaginings, she hugged them tight all the way home.

42

DAX LIMPED HIS WAY UP CARRALL STREET THEN ACROSS EAST HASTINGS, eventually finding a bench at Pigeon Park. He looked around for people he recognized, but saw few. It seemed like less old faces, but a lot of new ones had come to take their place. He remembered the years he had spent there, as they came rushing back at him in waves. Some memories are welcomed, while others intrude on one's thoughts like a thief in the night.

Just then, a large man in a trench coat and cowboy boots sat beside him. "What? It's getting hot over there," the man said accusingly.

"Some cop bitch is sniffing around," Dax said as he spit out in front of him.

"What's Spencer's plan?" the man asked lighting a cigar. "Get rid of her, I guess," Dax said, scanning the crowd.

"How's it going around here?" Dax asked.

"Same as it ever was, brother. Pain and wasting's on full tilt. Start wherever you want. Go see Cookie up the block for your gear," the man said as he stood up and walked away, exhaling smoke over his shoulder as he did it

Dax's eyes lit up; he was excited with the taste of death in his mouth. Victoria was so uptight and spread thin. This was where a man could really spread his wings. This was his kind of place. More junkies per square inch than anywhere in the country, and a city with its eyes closed tight to what happened here. It was heaven to him, and his ladies would have plenty of company tonight.

43

GLORIA GOT EVERY SNIPPET OF FOOTAGE SHE COULD FIND, BUT SHE STILL couldn't find a pattern that would show that Kate was stalked that night. All she had was a tape of a man with a limp coming up Caledonia and going down the alley behind Kate. The footage of the cruiser ended right as it crept up Quadra behind the trees, it disappeared after that. She packed up her gear and headed to her car. It was dark and the parking lot was surprisingly empty. She climbed into her car and stared at the spot where Kate had found Maya outside the Arena. Gloria looked at sidewalks and backyards a lot different than most people in the city. When she looked at a park, she thought of the bodies she had pulled out of there or some pursuit for a suspect that ended there. The map of the city for her was constantly changing, and it was never for the better.

'No wonder people move away when they retire,' she thought. 'Schoolteachers don't have to deal with this shit.' She never saw the saves anymore; she only saw the tragedy. She was told early on that when all you see are criminals and tragedy, it's time to move on. She thought of how much it was going to cost to put Amanda through school, and she winced. Amanda was going to be something else. 'No more cops in the family,' she thought.

Just then, a woman came out screaming and naked out of the Arena. Gloria's eyes focused to take in the sight. The woman squatted in front of a tree in the parking lot. Gloria saw the embarrassed faces of the staff, who followed her out. Apparently, this was the woman Gloria kept hearing about. Some psych staff had just dumped her at the Arena with no papers and no meds and just expected that she would blend in. She started causing disturbances as soon as everyone in the Arena started to run out of dope, sometime near welfare day. Here she was for all to see. Gloria looked at the buildings surrounding the parking lot and shook her head.

'These people are constantly calling,' she thought. Then a small still voice whispered, 'Imagine what it's like to live in there.' Chills ran down Gloria's spine as she called for backup. They would put the woman in the drunk tank for a time. What else could they do? They weren't social workers or doctors, they were police. The doctors dumped her here. That was the part that never seemed to sit right with Gloria or any cop, really. If these doctors and social work types were so high and mighty with their caring degrees and that vow to do no harm, then what was this? An Arena full of people being treated like animals, and hospitals that threw these people out as soon as they arrived.

The police were always phoned immediately to escort the homeless and addicted off of hospital property. If Welfare was poverty management, then the Health Authority was death management. Gloria drove home shaking her head. 'What is this all about?' she thought. A pandemic without sick people. A health management system without a soul. A force protecting them…

43

Murdoch: *Are you back home?*

Kate: *YES*

Murdoch: *I'll be there soon.*

KATE'S ANTICIPATION MADE HER HEAT UP AND START TO SWEAT. SHE started looking around for cleaner clothes to wear and really started to question her whole wardrobe in the process. When the knock came on the door, she was standing in front of the closet with two shirts in her hands and one around her neck. She quickly went to the door with the original situation on, checking her hair in the mirror before she opened the door.

Kate unlocked the door, made sure it was him, and then quickly turned around and walked into the living room to hide her blushing red cheeks. She didn't blush often, but when she did, it was all the worse because it was a new color on her. She turned and faced him as he came down the hallway. His presence was ominous. He seemed to fill the whole space when he entered it. She sat down on the couch farthest from him and tried to act nonchalant, playing with her hair awkwardly and scanning the room for refuse. She spotted a sock directly below the chair he sat on and she rolled her eyes. "How are you feeling?" he said looking around the room as he settled in.

"I'm much better; the dizziness has mostly gone away," Kate said feeling her forehead to see if she was still sweating.

"I couldn't find him, but I got people out looking for him," he said looking at her. His concern for her made her take a deep breath. She felt for that moment that nothing had happened and she was transported back to that place with him. "I found something else out too," he said as she was actively, not really listening.

She was thinking of asking him about Guillermo, the bulldog. She wanted to ask him so many things, but she just listened to him instead. "What?" Kate said.

"We are getting our dope from the Dorian Brothers Group," he said.

"Who is that?" Kate asked confused.

"It's the development company that did the hospital a number of years back. They are also actively involved in a number of sites around Pandora," he said looking over at her.

"What does it mean?" Kate asked.

"They launder money through development projects is what it means, and they are the ones responsible for the blackout down there."

Kate's head started tingling from the news. All those connections from before started swirling around in her head. For fifteen years, the city had been pushing people from Pandora down into L Street. This pandemic was the perfect opportunity to move them once and for all. It was like a military operation: First you turn off the lights. Then you remove sanitation, stop disinfecting the street, deny bathrooms and showers to people, close all stores that provide service to poor people (the fast food joint across the street was only allowing drive-thru customers), and then you defund the police under the guise that everyone would be staying home anyways.

You let the people out on the street fend for themselves. Give everyone down there a tent and a CERB cheque and increase the potency of the dope while dropping the price. Follow that up with hourly news reports on how bad the pandemic will be to get the fear up to maximum levels to increase drug use. After a month, give 30% of the people who survive the first wave of attacks hotel rooms down towards L Street, for appearances. Displace the rest to the parks and down the street to Centennial Square. Then erect fences all around Pandora and do hourly sweeps to clean the homeless off the block. All the while, build two huge condo towers right beside the homeless shelter. Kate felt sick to her stomach.

"Are you okay?" Murdoch asked.

"Ya, I just get sick in the morning," she said as she held her stomach. A wave of fear came over her as she said it. 'What if he knows?' she thought. She turned from his gaze in fear.

"Well, thanks for coming to see me," she said embarrassed with the color starting to fill her cheeks again.

"Text me if you need anything," he said, not being quite sure what to do.

She stood up and walked him to the door. The two of them barely fit in the hallway. He put his hand on her back, and she felt her hands stop shaking. She turned to him, and he pulled her close. She buried her head into his chest and took a deep breath, his smell filling her nostrils. She suddenly felt light-headed, so she leaned against the wall beside the door.

"Bye," he said as he walked out the door. She exhaled as she closed the door. How was she ever going to tell him? 'What am I going to do?' she thought. She quickly went and laid down. The smell of him was all over her. She fell asleep for a while, thinking of him and a baby. She had never felt this way before. Sure, she had imagined being a mother, but never like this. It was like she was being controlled by it; every thought lead back to it. She thought about the block and all the people there too. What was she going to do?

44

SPRING SEEMED TO COME AND GO WITHOUT NOTICE AS THE CITY WAS actively locked down. June saw the highest amount of opiate deaths in the history of the opiate crisis. The health authority opened the safe injection site the day after the news. There wasn't anybody on the block to go in though; they had all been cleared off. There had been other stories too. Like the guy who got out of prison and tried to use at a number of safe injection sites around town and had been turned away. He died of an overdose when he got back to his hotel.

There was so many missing people and deaths that it left a fog over the population. It was a confusing time for everyone in the city. The crime rate had risen in the neighborhoods where the homeless people were housed in hotels, while the other homeless people who weren't so lucky just slept outside or snuck in and out of the buildings. There was lots of pushback from neighborhoods as petitions were passed around, and pressure was applied to the city for action. The people who had the most in common with the homeless population and were closest to them in socio-economic status made it hardest for them. The old adage was: "You can always hire half of the poor to police and kill the other half."

45

A MAN SAT OUTSIDE AN APARTMENT BUILDING DOWNTOWN EYEING THE front door and possible exits. He watched a tall biker type leave by way of the front door, step into a waiting car, and speed away. He would wait for dark. He had been busy though. June hadn't had the highest overdose rate in history by accident. As soon as he got tapped to come over on the ferry, he had planned a diabolical scheme to gather as many souls as he could. This was going to be biblical.

He had succeeded where the others had failed. He just had one more thing to do: Kill this woman inside the apartment, and then he was gone. She hadn't come out since she arrived a few days earlier. He would have gotten her in the hospital if there wasn't so many witnesses. He was patient. He had time. He had a taste for the hunt. He usually just dosed unsuspecting parasites. It was a rare opportunity to take one so young, so beautiful. He relished the opportunity. The union had nicknamed him the "Taker" and that is exactly what he was here to do.

47

GLORIA LOOKED THROUGH EVERY CASE SPENCER HAD BEEN INVOLVED with – those that she could find, that is. He had been pretty busy since 2001 in counter terrorism, human trafficking, and narcotics. She was trying to find the case that turned him. She knew every cop had a breaking point. She had seen it. Sometimes when a cop has seen too much of the 7%, they become them. 7% was the magic number of the population the police dealt with on a regular basis. Always those same 7%, over and over again.

Spencer was no different than anyone else except he had seen and met more than most. Still, it didn't make any sense. Why would he go so far? She knew he had been married a number of times and had lots of debt because of his kids. Could it be money? She started trying to get financials for him through administration and found that his wages had been garnished. He was broke. She dug further and found that he had declared bankruptcy two years ago. As she scrolled up and down the file, she couldn't help seeing most of the cops she knew. They worked horrific cases for meager pay and usually supported a number of people. She knew this man's situation well, had seen it all her life. The first wife takes half the pension, and the second wife takes it all. She now had enough to go to Internal Affairs. She would go in the morning. She would like to see them folks down there while they were crisp. They had a lot to discuss. She had little evidence linking him to the overdoses but plenty of motive. She would play her hand in the morning.

48

KATE TOSSED AND TURNED IN A COLD SWEAT; THE PILLS SHE WAS ON MADE her drift in and out of consciousness. She was deep within a dream when she noticed that the bathroom light was off. She drifted off again down the river of unconsciousness. The pills made everything feel heavy. She felt a weight on her chest, and she slid her back along the mattress to adjust out of it, but it wouldn't move. She struggled in her sleep to get out from underneath it, but she couldn't. She felt trapped under its weight. She swallowed hard and opened her eyes. It was at that moment she felt her shoulders press into the mattress. There was something on top of her, but she couldn't see. Her breathing started to quicken as a bag was pulled over her head. She struggled as she felt the restriction of the panic breaths she was now taking. She smelt something recognizable. It smelled like work. Her breath calmed and her eyes rolled back in her head. The bag was pressed over her face, and she began to gag. She heard a loud BOOM and then muffled voices as she drifted off. She started breathing but lost consciousness.

Kate woke up in a panic, taking deep breaths. There were bright lights above her from her room and all sorts of faces staring at her. They all cheered as she came into focus on them. "Welcome back! We thought we had lost you," a voice said to her as Kate's eyes darted back and forth. "You had an overdose, but you are okay now," the voice explained as Kate's breathing got heavy and she felt like puking. They rolled her off the bed, and she sat on the ground with the bed behind her back. She could see syringe wrappers and empty bottles of cracked Narcan capsules on the ground.

There was lots of commotion going on behind her, but she could not see. All she could see were the shadows on the wall. She tried to make out the commotion and even turn around, but she couldn't move. Every move made her feel nauseous. She tried to swallow, but it was hard. She felt dizzy. Just then, she heard a familiar voice come into her earshot. She couldn't quite make it out, but it moved fast through the apartment.

"Are you okay?" a voice said from above Kate.

Kate looked up and it was Gloria. "I don't know," Kate said staring at her with her little feet pressed up against the wall.

"Can you stand up?" Gloria said forcing Kate to rise up to a sitting position on the bed. All at once, Gloria lifted Kate up to her feet and they took a few steps towards the living room. Kate looked left and saw blood all over her bed and a body face first on it. She screamed. All of her emotions came rushing back to her. The weight... It had been a person. She took panic breaths again and barely made it to the couch. The door was shut to her room, and she suddenly noticed the flashing amber and blue lights through her apartment windows from the street.

"What happened?!" Kate asked. The color had completely left her face.

"A man broke in here and had you pinned down to the bed when he was shot, it looked like he was trying to poison you. You overdosed, and the officers on the scene gave you Narcan," Gloria informed her. "I had left a couple of men on a detail to watch you. They saw the assailant break in. You're very lucky," Gloria continued.

Kate was completely astonished. In a flash instant she remembered the baby and she started to cry. She cried for a long time it seemed, as Gloria rubbed her shoulders. Her face was completely drenched, and the tears ran all over her hands as she kept wiping them away. She cried long and hard as if she were alone. She just let go.

49

GLORIA WALKED INTO INTERNAL AFFAIRS EARLY THAT MORNING WITH A file under one arm and a coffee in her hand. She didn't expect that she had enough to nail Spencer, but she had enough to get an inquiry. After the night she just had, she was juiced to catch all these guys. They ran the prints from the dead body and it turned out that the perp was Rob Jeffries. He had a long rap sheet of sexual assaults going back to his teens. He was well known within the system but mostly operated in the East End of Vancouver. He had bound Kate's arms to the bed and was suffocating her with a plastic bag after administering a high dose of fentanyl to her in her sleep. She had overdosed instantly and was gasping her last breath when he was shot.

Gloria could feel the momentum swinging in her favor, and she walked with a swagger through their offices. She was welcomed by their secretary and left to sit in a boardroom and wait for the Director of Operations. She scrolled through her phone looking for the story on the news, when the Director and two aides came in the room. The morning was long for her in that room. She had a lot of speculation but some tangible leads. She was commended on her great work and assured that an investigation was underway. When she got out of the building, the news was playing the story everywhere. Kate had been moved to a safe location, so she was far away from the news crews that now lined her street. Gloria felt vindicated as she walked out to her car. The bright light from the sunny morning filled her eyes with hope.

50

SOMEWHERE ALONG CARRALL STREET THE NEWS PASSED, AND A PHONE call rang in Dax's ears. "Ya," Dax said to the voice on the other end of the line. "I saw it. I know…I will." The phone hung up, and Dax let out a deep breath. He was summoned. He knew what this meant. He rubbed the pipe in his breast pocket as he headed towards the sky train. He put a skull mask on as he limped down the street, and all of hell followed with him.

51

KATE LAY IN BED TRYING TO SLEEP, BUT ALL SHE COULD GET WAS SHORT naps. She was terrified of deep sleep and what waited for her down there. She had been moved to an unknown address, way out of town, somewhere in Sooke. She couldn't even use her phone. Gloria told her that all her contacts were compromised. Gloria said Murdoch could be one of the men trying to hurt her. When Kate heard that, she was shocked by the notion. But after further deliberating, she asked herself: 'How well do I really know this guy? How did they meet and what is the basis of their communication? She started to draw multiple connections across time laced with paranoia. She couldn't trust anyone anymore. She didn't remember having many good friends to begin with. Most of her friendships faded when she kept taking Manny back, and the rest faded when she left school.

She kept feeling the weight of that man on her chest when she layed down. She wouldn't take the pain meds because it re-created the feelings from the overdose. Days slipped away. Her body was numb, and her mind was detached. She kept wondering if that had really happened. She couldn't believe that Murdoch would do this to her. She felt she would rather die than know that was true. She felt lost, but she didn't want to be found. She felt indifferent, but deep emotion surrounded her, ready to rush in at any time. She couldn't take the thought of going back to her apartment or her old life, but then she would be planning each step of her return to it. She seemed to be two people: one was desperately trying to escape and the other was actively planning a siege.

The Opiate Murders

Just then Gloria entered the house. Kate shuddered when the door opened. "How are you doing?" Gloria asked as she sat down at the table and took out her notepad.

"I'm alright," Kate responded as she lit a cigarette. Probably the only real comfort she had found in her new surroundings was smoking.

"I got some more things from your place; your mom picked them out," Gloria said.

"When can I see her?" Kate said accusingly.

"I know this is hard, but we just want you to be safe," Gloria reassured her.

"Why the fuck can't I have my phone?" Kate yelled. She was sick of this situation and all the safety precautions.

"We don't know how they knew where you lived, Kate. I can't risk you being found again – not until this is over," Gloria tried to level with her.

"Till what's over!? These people run the whole city. Murdoch told me the developers gave them pure fentanyl when the dope ran out and told them to look the other way on Pandora," Kate said crossing her arms in disgust. She sat up anticipating a fight.

"What developers?" Gloria asked.

"The Dorian Brothers first of all, and probably a bunch of others," Kate exclaimed.

"You can't trust him, Kate, he was the last person to see you before the incident," Gloria reminded her in a low, concerned voice. She had seen witnesses lose it before; she didn't want Kate to take off.

"Why don't you go check it out before you start accusing Murdoch of anything," Kate snapped.

"Check out where?" Gloria said at a loss for words.

"It's plain as day. They are building two massive buildings right beside the homeless shelter and probably renovating the building on the other side. Isn't that a motive?" Kate was shaking now. Fighting for her point had made her come alive, but she was instantly tired from it.

"That's not enough, Kate," Gloria said offhandedly.

"That's the problem isn't it? You're all connected. Who shut down the safe injection site? Not you, but you know who did. Who cleared the block? You did, but who did you do it for? Who stopped collecting garbage and sanitizing the street? You know. Who brought in the killer fentanyl when the dope ran out? I know, but you won't believe it. It's your fucking people!" Kate yelled.

"How do you know these things for sure, Kate?" Gloria said finally after a long pause.

"I watched them happen, and I almost got killed for it," Kate said in a low, aggressive tone.

Gloria looked into her eyes and felt faint. Gloria knew a lot of what Kate was saying was true. It was just that nobody ever talked about it. On the force you did your job and blocked out the rest. The city was built a certain way, and people were managed another. She never saw them as the same. She had been on many details raising people from their tents in the morning. She knew what it was to send people off into the unknown. It wasn't her problem; it was her job, and there was a difference. She kept her feelings about it inside. That's how one advanced on the force.

She saw Kate staring back at her and thought about all she had been through. She had read the file about Manny. She knew Kate had woken up with him dead beside her. Gloria knew the kind of road Kate was on after that attack. Gloria had been attacked numerous times in her career. It never goes away. You're always looking over your shoulder, and the one time you don't, some crazy guy kills you in front of a 7-Eleven. That had happened to a friend of Gloria's a couple years back. She thought about her every day.

"Kate, I know this has been hard for you, but I'm a cop. There is no great conspiracy behind it all, trust me." Gloria tried to reassure her with what she knew so well.

Kate lit another cigarette and got real quiet. "Do you know why that guy tried to kill those people at the Arena?" Kate said after she took a long drag off her smoke.

"I don't," Gloria said.

"Because you're all in on it, and you don't even know it. You don't care about these people. I do, and that's why they are trying to kill me and not you." Kate was furious. Her eyes dilated and she leaned forward and whispered, "They know where I am. You aren't protecting me. You never could because you are the same people who put me here."

Gloria stood up and walked out of the house.

'Who the fuck does this girl think she is? We saved her fucking life,' Gloria thought. She got in her car and started driving back to the city. The whole story came to her in violent images. First the shutdown and how the bodies started to pile up. The smell of that street. The violence that followed the shutdown. The hotels and the clearing of the block. The absence of any and all sick people in the population. The construction sites working at full capacity the whole time. Kate in the hospital. Spencer telling her off at the base. The shooting of an East End parasite, trying to kill a witness in her home… The search for a homegrown opiate killer.

52

WHENEVER THERE IS A LOSS WITHIN THE BROTHERHOOD, THEY RELEASE what they like to call "Red Death", which just translates as "bad dope". There were eighteen overdoses that week. Six in one of the hotels in one day. It killed nine people the first week, just in Victoria. Vancouver was much worse. The Province extended the drug advisory for opiate use again, claiming all the same things: stagger your use, don't use alone, etc. The thing that nobody had figured out till Kate had was: What if these people who died weren't using alone? What if one of the brotherhood was with them? Gloria was knee-deep into all of it.

Internal Affairs arrested Mike Spencer on charges of corruption. His finances were linked to a number of the Dorian Brothers' subsidiaries. They had co-signed a loan for him after his bankruptcy amongst various other transfers of large sums of cash to offshore accounts. Apparently, Internal Affairs and Interpol were pretty bored during the lockdown; they dedicated a whole squad to nailing Spencer. Many other cops either resigned or were picked up that week. It fell like dominos. A pipe that the 'Taker' had on him the night he tried to kill Kate was traced to six overdose deaths in Victoria alone during the month of June. Forensics was cross-referencing it against overdose deaths in the East End.

All in all, July and August passed by quickly because the whispers of a second wave were everywhere. Not bad enough to clear out every toilet paper aisle in town, but the trepidation was definitely there. People were seen walking around outside with masks on or driving in their cars alone with one on. People even jogged outside with a mask on. Strange times they were, and as September began, there was all sorts of passive-aggressive two-steps going on all over town. Literally, nobody knew where to stand.

As the rain started to come down, there was a cooling of the population. It seemed as if a part of their soul had been cleansed. Nobody wanted to be outside anymore. Everyone got that hint of fall that comes over you when the sun starts to go down earlier, and it's dark all of a sudden when it used to be light. The leaves started to fall everywhere, and the energy shifted from patios to Halloween decorations.

53

KATE SAT INSIDE HER HIDEOUT AND WATCHED THE RAIN COME DOWN THE window. She was three months pregnant now, and she felt a human forming inside her every day. She started to feel herself missing someone she had never met. She agonized about it. She cried a lot alone in that house. She had gotten a new phone with a new number, but she hadn't contacted Murdoch. She wouldn't believe that he had been involved with the incident. Gloria hadn't proved anything about him except that he had been to her house. She longed to speak with him but didn't know how. She was being watched twenty-four hours a day.

She didn't want to get him into trouble. She thought about how many children grow up without a father. She never imagined that she would be having a child and least of all with a man like him. Maybe she wouldn't ever tell him. He would just go on with his life and have some faint distant memory of her. "Oh ya, Kate," he would say. "I knew a girl like that once," and that would be the end of it. He would spend his life doing what he always did, and every day his child would do what they did. The two of them could pass on the street and not know who each other was. She bet that happened a lot.

'This world seems to want to split us apart and make us all strangers,' she thought. She imagined all the scenarios in which she would run into him where she wouldn't tell him, and then she would run the scenarios where she did. Sometimes she would imagine his face lighting up. Sometimes she would imagine him screaming at her in the street. Once she imagined tears streaming from his eyes. She liked that one the best. That was only on a good day though. There weren't many of those for her, not lately.

The Opiate Murders

Kate had no idea when or if she was going back to her old life. She heard talk of her maybe moving to the interior or Ontario even. Witness protection was no joke, but it wasn't like on TV, where they whisked you away to a non-disclosed location by yourself. She had to share the house with a detail of cops. Men mostly, who avoided her and didn't let her leave. It was like living with the masculine archetype. They came in, made coffee, went to the bathroom, and never talked to her. She felt like she was in a polyamorous relationship without any sex or sister wives to talk to. And she was pregnant. So pregnant. She could eat the handle off the fridge door if they let her.

Her only joy was going to Costco to pick out food and clothing. She would stay there for hours. The cops had a special deal where she could go in there after closing time and spend one hour inside unsupervised and shop with no real limit. Well, maybe there was a limit. She tried to bring home a patio set once with a fireplace, and she wasn't allowed. Beyond that she could get anything within reason. She had enough strawberry cheesecake to kill a kindergarten class. Boredom in the downtime revolved around going for walks around Sooke with her brother husbands and watching daytime television.

She really hated it when they didn't find out who the father was on those shows where five men are sitting up on stage with a woman and the baby. She thought it must be one of them, and then it turned out to be none of them. 'OMG. What a nightmare!' she thought. She never had any sympathy for these women before, now she was in a whole other world. She felt she had more in common with every mother than any other woman. Now there was a huge difference. Women had no skin in the game; mothers were all in. September came and went for Kate. The bump bumped and time marched on.

54

GLORIA WAITED FOR A PHONE CALL SITTING IN HER CAR IN A PARKING LOT adjacent to the safe injection site. She was waiting for the morgue to tell her what overdoses matched the Taker's pipe. "Hello?" Gloria said. "Yes!?" and then another resounding "Yes!" came out of Gloria before the phone call was done. That pipe had been linked to twelve overdose deaths in the East End of Vancouver. In her excitement, a chill ran right through her; it was like all those souls passed through her in celebration. She felt all of them and suddenly a tear came into her eye. She felt the kind of triumph, only a beer in a bar could quench. It was only ten in the morning, but she knew one bar that was open.

As she pulled up to her dad's house, she put her phone on silent and left her gun and everything in the car. She came in through the basement as usual. "Hey, Dad. Why isn't the game on? There has to be a game on somewhere!" she said as she climbed the stairs.

When she reached the top of the stairs, her dad was sitting in a chair facing the TV that was on mute. He had a blanket over his head. "What? Did you fall asleep out here?" Gloria asked as she pulled the blanket away. Gloria slowly sank to her knees beside him as she absorbed the sight of him. Her father's face was white as snow and his lips were dark blue, almost black. He was dead.

A toxicology screen showed opiate, fentanyl, and benzos. There was no sign of false entry, and no torch or paraphernalia to show that he had been using. Just a dead man without a tale to tell and even less evidence to go by. Gloria screamed at the detectives when they asked if he had a drug problem. "Don't you know what this is?!" she screamed.

The Opiate Murders

"I'm sorry. We have to ask these questions. We know he lived alone. Did he ever have any company? Maybe female, maybe an escort?" the detective asked.

"Fuck off. I can't do this right now." Gloria stormed out of the house to her car. She scream cried with her head in the middle of the steering wheel; it even honked once. She was startled and was rattled back into the world by the sound. She looked up, all at once through all the paramedics and cops surrounding the house, she knew what to do.

She started her car and drove away. All the way down to the precinct, it felt like someone else was driving. She wondered when the grief would kick in or was this it? She parked her car outside the station and turned on her computer. 'These killers were cowards,' she thought. 'How could they get in the house with no forced entry and do that to him?'

Her head spun from the thoughts that seemed to seize her from without. Her bewilderment became a deep sadness and a longing for her mother. She never really knew her mother because she had died so young, but whenever Gloria was lost and alone, she would miss her the most. Inside Gloria's world, her mother could always fix everything. Gloria thought about the funeral they had for her mother and how her dad had cried once everyone went home, and it was just the two of them. She thought about Amanda and how she would take it. It must have been a few hours before Gloria noticed that the engine was running. She put the car into gear and drove home. Her plan would have to wait.

55

THE HEADLINES READ: "TOP COP DIES OF DRUG ASPHYXIATION". IT WAS A massive funeral. The army was there, social distanced on a lawn. The death had caught nationwide coverage. Gloria was bombarded by the press for interviews. She still wouldn't talk to the detectives. She took her daughter to a cabin up in Tofino and sat by the ocean. The place was deserted. She had never seen it like that. The waves crashed against the beach alone without any Chinese tourists running around taking pictures.

Gloria still kept tabs on Kate. She would call at least once a day to annoy her. Kate was getting along just fine. She was mostly sorry about the tragedy. She even thought it might be her fault somehow, but Gloria made sure that Kate knew it had nothing to do with her. A week had passed since the funeral when Gloria decided to come back. Amanda missed her friends, and Gloria felt like she was going stir crazy. She decided to take Kate out when she got back. She had no idea how bad all that sitting around could get. Gloria thought she gained ten pounds that week.

When Gloria got back, she walked the site with the detectives and told them everything. She cried in her car after that for an hour. She just couldn't escape the guilt she felt. She hadn't talked to him for years, it seemed. She went there with good news. The whole time she was celebrating on the way there, he was dying. She sobbed pitifully at the thought of it all. How could she ever get ahead of this?

'Where the fuck are these guys?' she thought. Then her plan came back to her. She had to draw them out. She knew they would be riding high but lying low. None of them would show their faces now. Gloria had the upper hand. They just didn't know it yet.

56

KATE SAT AT THE KITCHEN TABLE, SIFTING THROUGH MAGAZINES THAT were brought to her by the fellas. Apparently, all their wives had put a care package together for Kate. She got a bunch of magazines ranging from *Cosmo* to *Vanity Fair*, lots of chocolate, and baby clothes. She was brimming with excitement when Gloria came pulling up.

Gloria talked for a time outside with the guys on Kate's detail. Kate watched Gloria through the window. She looked different to Kate somehow. She was always a very attractive lady, but since her father's death, her face had hardened, and her hair had darkened. Her eyes shone black when she stared into the sun. The air had gotten colder as October was coming to a close, and the leaves had fallen and changed colors. Against the black in Gloria's eyes, a glimmer of orange flashed, and Kate adjusted her eyes to focus on it. Kate was afraid, but she didn't want to show it.

Gloria came into the house a few moments later and sat across the table from Kate, studying the pile of gifts strewn across the table. "Quite the haul you got here," Gloria said as she flipped through one of the magazines. "One of the guys says that there might be a few *Playboys* in here because he can't find his." Kate and Gloria laughed a bit, and Kate got less nervous.

"I was looking to organize a memorial at Beacon Hill Park for all the victims of the opiate crisis. A candlelight vigil from 6:00 p.m. to 6:00 a.m. on November 2nd," Gloria said with a probing tone.

"The day of the dead," Kate said as her eyes flashed and met with Gloria's.

"The only thing I'm worried about is the drug use," Gloria said with a tone of faint concern. "Have you ever been to an overdose funeral?"

"Half the people there are high, and the younger the crowd, the higher they are," Kate said straightening herself out in the chair and ignoring the magazine. "The only other problem I can see is the social distancing."

Gloria raised an eyebrow. Kate's eyes gleamed, and she took control of the conversation. "First of all, we will only have deaths from the block honored, so there won't be any sixteen-year-old first time fatality deaths being honored. They can save that for Centennial Square and the news crews. Second, we will be having it after six when everyone is safe at home in their living rooms. Nobody cares about these homeless people, and if that isn't enough, me and you both know that nobody in the homeless population ever got sick in Victoria, and they never could social distance, so?"

Kate looked across the table and crossed her arms and rolled her eyes. It was a fact that the numbers in Victoria were so low that it was embarrassing. At the end of September there had been forty-six cases of COVID reported in seven months with two deaths. There had been one hundred plus overdose deaths in Victoria in 2020.

Gloria sat there for a moment and took a deep breath. "Can you come?" Gloria asked finally.

"You want to draw them out!?" Kate said with her eyes widening to meet with the possibility of excitement. She was so bored that even a whisper of a thrill made her salivate. She was used to the heavy action from the block or even the Arena. This sitting around was killing her.

"We will be everywhere; you will be protected," Gloria reassured her.

"This is awesome. I'm so glad you are doing this."

Kate and Gloria were both relieved by the exchange. Kate was relieved because for the longest time she had the sneaking suspicion that the cops were going to cover all this up, especially after the round-up of cops following Spencer's arrest and then Gloria's dad's death. Kate was reinvigorated by all the possibilities this new venture held. Kate was excited and terrified… She was loving it. Gloria looked across the table and felt that feeling of guilt and grief begin to ease. She had found a viable solution to end this once and for all.

57

THE ONLY PROBLEM WITH ORGANIZING A CANDLELIGHT VIGIL WAS THAT Gloria needed the homeless population to organize it, and they were spread out all over the city. How was she going to get the word out to all of them and then convince them to go? She was going to need someone from the population that she could trust; someone that wouldn't give her secret away.

She went right to Bobby Jay. Bobby Jay was an all arounder. He had been on the street for the last fifteen years. When Gloria asked him why he didn't get one of the hotels he said, "I was too busy getting fucked up." He was perfect. He knew most of the people who had died and many who had been forgotten over the years. He was going to gather an army. Bobby went from hotel to camp and then back downtown until the word was out that there was a party at Beacon Hill Park for the overdose victims. "Bring as much dope as you can, and he would bring as much gear as he could find!" Kate worked on getting backpacks of gear for the event.

The candles and pictures were supplied by various advocacy groups against homelessness across the city. They also got their hands on a ton of makeup from some of the local businesses and tattoo artists were going to donate their time to painting people's faces for the event. The neighborhood even welcomed the event after they were told that the park would be guarded all night long by security and crews would clean up the next day. It was all happening, and the city started to fill with a buzz. You could feel it everywhere you went, from Pandora to the Gorge. Campers at certain parks moved completely out and back to Beacon Hill for it. As Halloween passed with its empty streets and virtual trick-or-treating happening inside, the outside came alive with shadows. They say that Halloween opens up a portal where the veil between this world and the next becomes thin. Gloria was hoping to summon the dead to come out and prey on the living one more time. She knew Dax and his people couldn't resist it. Gloria would have fifty officers in every walk of life in that park waiting for them.

58

ON THE MORNING OF NOVEMBER 2ND, CREWS OF PEOPLE DESCENDED INTO Beacon Hill to prepare for the event. Social distancing was set up so everywhere there was seating, like in the theatre, in the middle of the park, where they would be showing slides and playing music. Every tree was adorned for a victim of the crisis. Each got a black sash and an orange sash across the tree with the picture of the victim and a candle underneath it. The tables were set for face painting, and various venders gave away free food and supplies during the day. There was a backlash on TV about gathering crowds, but anybody attached to the event knew that was just posturing by the ineffectual populace trying to highjack the event for their own agendas.

The homeless populations started moving in to check out the event as early as the day before. Kate and her contacts got as many dealer's and supplies to the park as possible so they could attract everyone they needed. By the time the event was under way, they were having decent numbers coming through the service areas. Mostly, people stayed away and congregated in small groups around certain areas. There were already lots of tents in Beacon Hill, so when it started to get dark, you could see shadows of people moving all around. This was it, and as it got darker, everyone sat back and waited for the shadows to come out into the light.

It was a sight to behold: small groups of people walking amongst the trees painted up like the dead. Some were high, some were really high, and the rest oscillated between states of pain and euphoria. The candles illuminated the faces of the victims of this crisis. There were so many. They didn't have enough trees. You would hear people crying out to them in the dark. Kate held hands with the people closest to her and cried. It was a great time of healing for her. At the very beginning of one of the trails was a picture of Gloria's dad. She had put it there. She wanted them to know she wasn't afraid of anything or anyone. She was waiting for them.

59

AS THE NIGHT WORE ON, KATE GOT TO SEE A LOT OF OLD FRIENDS AND maybe even some that weren't her friends. They were all gathered together to honor something bigger than themselves: Death. It seemed to be the one thing that had been missing from the pandemic rhetoric. The one thing that everyone has in common that nobody can escape. It was something that had been collectively lost, as the population seemed scared of its existential fate. The fact that we live in a death-denying society was exposed during the pandemic. Nobody is allowed to die of anything, at any age. It seemed that standing out there amongst those people released that collective fear. It made them whole again. Like knowing your mortality could heal you.

As the night passed, the mid-point people started to disappear. It was cold outside, and people retreated to the warmth of their tents. Kate walked over to the bathroom and headed in. The stalls had been social distanced, so she picked the one that was closest to the sinks. She sat down on a very cold seat and checked quickly for paper. The silence was deafening in there as she dreaded the sound of anyone who might be coming in. She finished and stood up, but as she flushed the toilet, she was sprayed in the face by something above her. Her knees buckled as she took a deep breath and slumped beside the toilet. She could feel a shuffle from the stall next to her as she began to lose consciousness. In that instant, she heard gunshots as she passed once again into oblivion.

60

GLORIA SPENT MOST THE NIGHT IN THE PERIPHERAL OF THE EVENT. SHE watched the comings and goings of people in masks. Anyone with a limp or a cane was tracked. The event was pretty quiet. People mostly came and went. It was dark and cold most of the night. There were five people tracking Kate. Two with her and three around her. She was with a number of people she knew as well, in the middle of the event most of the night. As midnight came and went, the park cleared out, and Gloria headed in to talk with Kate. Nobody had come out. They would have to try something else. As she approached the group, she was told that Kate had gone to the bathroom. That is when she heard the shots. Three quick gunshots from over by the bathroom.

Gloria ran towards a group that ran away from that direction. She pushed them out of the way as she ran. When she got to the bathrooms, two officers stood over a man who was on the ground and the bathroom was full of people. Kate was being massaged around the neck by the point person, administered Narcan by the secondary, and the third was calling the ambulance. She watched Kate start gasping for air as she came back to life. Kate immediately rubbed her stomach and started to say, "I'm okay; he's okay."

Gloria knelt beside her and held Kate's hand. "I didn't know you knew it was a boy," Gloria said.

"I don't," Kate returned. When the ambulance arrived, Kate walked out to it and drove away. Gloria followed. Apparently, the guy on the ground wasn't Dax. They were checking the database to find an identity. The two cops from her detail put him down as he was running out of the bathroom. They thought the bathroom was clear when they swept it a moment before. One of the men resigned after the event. They found a spray can on the perp that was filled with pure fentanyl. The incident went unreported because it was part of an ongoing investigation. All that was said was that there was an overdose incident that was cleared up and that the pops heard were fireworks. Kate left the hospital almost immediately that night and headed back to her compound with her heart still pounding from the event.

61

EARLY MORNING SUNSHINE ILLUMINATED THE HIGHWAY TO SOOKE AS Gloria sped along anxiously to check up on Kate. Guilt consumed her as she thought of the incident over and over again. Nobody would ever have thought to check in the ceiling for the guy. She kept going back in her mind, imagining what she could have done to make it different. She ached to know how the baby was. 'Why the fuck did you do this Gloria!' she screamed at herself as she pulled the car over to the side of the road.

She thought about the body in the morgue and agonized over it not even being Dax. 'How many of these fucking guys are there?!' she screamed inside her head. She watched a couple of cars speed by her, and she started to gain her composure. She put the car into gear and got back into formation with herself and the road. She had taken a shot, and it didn't work out. That was the job. She had no time to go back and do it differently because that time had passed. All she had was what was in front of her.

Halloween pumpkins still lined the roads as she drove into the town and then into the compound. She drove up to the house and got out of the car. She could see that everyone was alert and awake; all the lights inside were on too, so she decided to go in. When Gloria stepped inside the house, Kate was sitting at the kitchen table eating ice cream.

"I thought we might as well live it up while we can," Kate said rubbing her tummy.

Gloria smiled and sat down. "Are you okay?" she asked, trying to conceal her shame.

"What kind of Day of the Dead would it be if you didn't die at least once?" Kate said, laughing it off.

"Seriously, what did the doctor say?" Gloria asked leveling the comedy for a second.

"They said he is fine," Kate said.

"You still think it's a boy?" Gloria said with a smile.

"Fuck ya, girl. I do now. He's going to be a soccer player," Kate said rubbing her tummy again and eating the rest of the ice cream.

Gloria took Kate's cell phone out of her pocket and slid it across the table.

"Seriously!?" Kate said as a huge smile came across her face.

"Just don't tell anyone where you are," Gloria said sternly.

"Thank you so much! I got a hankering for an app," she said as she powered it up.

"Kate, I am so sorry for putting you in that position. We had no idea that it would turn out the way it did," Gloria said looking at the ground in shame.

Kate looked up at her for a moment and then looked back down at her belly. "I have to apologize to you, actually, for saying that you are all in on it. I was mad, and it seemed at the time that things were too connected for it not to be everyone, but I was wrong. You guys are doing the best you can. I never thought in a million years that creep would be hiding up there. That shit was next level," Kate said looking above her with her eyes wide, and then she let out a fake scream. They both laughed uneasily. Gloria made a cup of coffee, and they both sat there and played on their phones until the sun had risen. Gloria started to feel like if she stayed even five more minutes she was going to need to sleep on the couch. Gloria said her goodbyes to Kate and her detail and drove home.

62

Kate: *Hey*

Murdoch: *Hey! I was worried about you!? Where have you been?*

Kate: *They took my phone away.*

Murdoch: *Are you ok?*

Kate: *Can we meet? Sooke potholes @12?*

Murdoch: *of course. C u then*

KATE HAD THOUGHT ABOUT WHAT SHE WAS GOING TO SAY TO HIM A THOUsand times, but it never got all the way to the end. She always imagined the house they would live in or the kind of clothes the baby would wear to match him. She thought she was losing her mind. 'When did she become such a lush?' she thought. 'The hormone game is no joke' she thought to herself as she watched Murdoch's truck pull into the parking lot.

Next thing she knew, she had a very excited bulldog running towards her. But just before Guillermo got to her, he stopped dead in his tracks and started barking at Kate's 'friends'. Sitting beside her and stationed beside her were three cops. She smiled as she rubbed Guillermo's head. "It's okay, bud. They are just for show."

She watched Murdoch walk slowly across the parking lot. She forgot how big he was. She started to feel warm all over. These hormones are no joke! she thought again.

The Opiate Murders

"Don't mind my friends here," Kate said as she patted one of her detail on the shoulder. She walked towards him and gave him a long hug. He put his hand on her back and the other one on the back of her head, holding her there for a moment. Then he took a deep breath. She hoped the moment would never end. But it did. They both felt the eyes on them, so they decided to take a walk. Guillermo growled as they walked by.

"Don't mind him, fellas. He don't like cops," Murdoch said as he took Kate's hand and walked with her towards the water.

When they got to the water, she turned to him and said, "I'm pregnant."

His head went back a little to meet the wave. He looked around for Guillermo and then looked back at her. "Okay," Murdoch said giving her a hug.

'Is that it?' Kate thought as they talked about some other things.

He explained that he had been worried sick when he heard someone tried to kill her, and then he couldn't reach her. She apologized. They skirted the baby topic, even though it was very obvious to him after she said it, because he immediately started to look at her stomach. She was scared at first to show him the bump, and she kept fussing with her clothes to hide it, but then suddenly, she just didn't care. She was amazingly comfortable with him. She was so small compared to him that she felt nothing about the bump. She never expected to feel this way.

They walked around a bit and eyed the people there for threats, but mostly people came there this time of the year to walk their dogs. Besides the occasional growl from the dogs that passed by, everything was peaceful. "When are you going to lose your entourage?" he asked in a low, serious tone.

Kate laughed as she spied them on the perimeter. "What? You don't like my henchmen?" Kate returned.

"I would like you to come stay with me," Murdoch said after a long pause. She liked that he never seemed to rush. He was very sure when he said something, like it was set in stone. He didn't second guess or speculate.

"They would never allow that," Kate said, sad at first, but then secretly liking not giving him what he wanted. She didn't remember any dates leading up to her just moving in. She wanted him to earn it. She laughed to herself, as the thoughts passed by in her mind.

"Where are you? Can I come see you?" Murdoch said, looking into her eyes. "I can't tell you," Kate said. She gave him a look of sadness, but secretly liked holding things from him.

'The push and pull of a man is tremendous,' she thought. She let his need and concern for her wash over her. This was way better than she could have ever imagined. She was scared of the feeling.

"I should go," Kate said as she bent down and petted Guillermo.

"I'll text you, now that I can," Murdoch said in a tone that conveyed his longing but also made the point that she better answer.

"I know," she said as she looked over her shoulder and watched him watch her walk away. She got into the unmarked black cruiser and sped off. Murdoch glared at the other car as it drove off behind her.

63

GLORIA PASSED OUT WHEN SHE GOT HOME AND DIDN'T WAKE UP AGAIN for sixteen hours. When she did wake, she was groggy and couldn't really think of anything in particular. She stood at the kitchen sink and made herself a coffee. She looked at a spotless kitchen counter and empty cupboards and wondered if anybody even lived there. Suddenly it all came flooding back to her: the shooting, the witness being attacked, and all those painted faces of the dead. She sat down and put the whole fiasco together in her head. She took a deep breath and looked out the window. Something at the back of her mind kept scratching at her for attention. She ignored it and finished her coffee. She ignored it and took a shower. She ignored it while she got dressed. She ignored it on the way out the door. She got in the car and couldn't ignore it anymore.

Gloria found herself sitting outside of a house with a manicured lawn in Sydney. Roger Paddick's house looked a little dismal in the November sun. The garden had lost its luster, and the trees had lost their leaves. She knocked on the door and got the dog. You know the type – small, purse-size with a woman attached to it.

"Oh, be quiet Bitzy," was all she heard. Roger came to the door abruptly. He looked shocked as he tried to tuck his shirt in and fix what was left of the hair on his head.

"Hello Gloria, I was sorry to hear about your dad. It's a real tragedy," he said catching his breath.

"Can we speak outside?" Gloria said quickly. She had something on her mind. When the two stepped outside, she condescendingly said, "Of course you heard about your friend Mike?" She wanted to get the balance of power flowing in her favor.

"Yes, that too was sad to hear" Roger averted her gaze as he said it.

"Funny how you can be on a guy's detail as long as you and not get any of that on you," Gloria said accusingly.

"Well, I wasn't with him every moment of the day," Roger said nonchalantly.

"I guess I'll just leave your comings and goings up to Internal Affairs then," Gloria returned, showing how serious this was. "Would hate to see a long career tarnished by the loss of your pension," she said after to sweeten the sting.

"I told you everything I knew before," Roger defended.

"You told me everything that lead away from you," Gloria finalized.

"I can't tell you something I don't know," Roger said at a loss.

"Maybe it's something you know that you don't think is important." Gloria coached him. "Mike was working pretty close with a few CI's. You must have known where and when he was meeting with them?" Gloria pressed.

"I didn't know because Mike didn't trust anyone, but I did hear about a place they would all use out in the West Shore," Roger said finally.

"Give me the address," Gloria said as she took a deep breath.

Roger disappeared into the house for a while and came back and handed her a piece of paper folded in half.

"Thanks for your time," Gloria said, snatching the piece of paper out of his hand. She watched him as she drove off. He looked like he was lost. She saw that look on a lot of men. They seemed to be living in a house they never wanted, tending to duties they never chose. Karma, it's sneaky, she thought.

64

GLORIA STAKED OUT THAT ADDRESS FOR A FEW DAYS AND EVEN PUT A detail on the place at night. She was about to give up on it when she saw something that she would never forget. A carpet cleaning van pulled up, and two men got out of it. One of them had a limp and a cane.

Gloria almost honked her horn with excitement. "No fucking way!" she said out loud. She watched the two men go in, then come out after a few minutes and drive away. Gloria pursued the van. She didn't call anyone or notify the dispatch. She didn't know how far the scope was on these guys. For all she knew, these guys could be working with another detail of cops. As she followed them, she was curious. Was this their day job? Seemed plausible. She was still in shock. It all seemed too easy; the way a task becomes old hat after you've mastered it.

The van pulled up to a building just off Jacklyn Road, and the two got out and went inside. Simple, it's the company address, she said to herself after looking it up. An hour went by and she looked off into the distance. She was getting tired, and her eyes were starting to hurt. She saw a flash in her peripheral vision, and she looked over to meet it. Dax was on a scooter driving off the property and down the road. She had almost missed it. The sun was going down as he sped towards the city, weaving in and out of traffic that was backed up between the lights. Gloria couldn't keep up without being noticed, and she lost him in a traffic jam on the highway. She circled the neighborhoods, but she couldn't find him anywhere. After cursing the fates, she settled down to the fact that she knew where he worked, and he had visited the address. She had him.

65

DAX'S REAL NAME WAS REGINALD SPEKTOR ON THE DATABASE FOR THE Carpet Cleaning business. He had been employed there for a number of years. Gloria also found that his company name was a subsidiary of the Dorian Brothers. She couldn't believe her luck. It all pieced itself together right in front of her eyes. She put a detail on the Carpet Cleaner and left one on the address in the West Shore. This was big. If she could nail the syndicate, they could put these guys out of business. She would read reports about addresses visited by Dax while he was working and when he was off work, where he stayed and who he met with.

Everything was going like clockwork until she got to work one morning and found her details had been pulled and her files were missing. Soon after, she was confronted by two agents from Internal Affairs in the hallway, who complimented her for her great work but told her that her case had been absolved into a larger investigation. She wasn't told what investigation. She was furious. She went to the Director of Operations, but he wouldn't see her. She staked out the addresses herself, but nobody came by.

Dax didn't go to work anymore; he didn't go anywhere. He was gone.

Gloria's head spun with rage. She was ready to shoot someone, when she got a call to come to the offices at the Legislature. She was to see the Minister of Security, Fire, and Police. She sat outside in the hallway and waited. After what seemed like a long time with her thoughts, she was confronted by the Minister and an entourage of TV reporters. She was awarded a medal of honor for the shooting of the suspect at the "Beacon Hill Park stakeout", as it was called. She was on the front

The Opiate Murders

page of the newspaper the next day. Nobody said a word about her other investigation, and she was redirected anytime she mentioned other crimes or criminals. She was even offered early retirement by the Minister himself. She couldn't believe it. The whole investigation was bumped up to some special prosecutor, and Gloria was back where she started.

66

GLORIA SAT IN HER CAR FACING THE SAFE INJECTION SITE ON PANDORA where it all started, watching a huge building site being erected right beside it. She couldn't believe her eyes. 'It is all connected,' she thought. It was like watching an anthill. She was a soldier ant, and across the street, they were all worker ants whether they were in the safe injection, homeless shelter, or erecting the building next door. She thought about the Queen down the hill at the Legislature, and she shook her head.

What could she do? She looked at the people who lined the street. The unfortunates, the vulnerable – they were the food that this anthill ran on. Dax and his crew were just the other side of the spectrum: soldier ants, the ones who worked in the shadows. Everyone was fulfilling their function; all pitted against each other, but at the same time working together. It all seemed so clear to her.

She had never seen it before because she didn't want to, she supposed. She spent a lot of her career running from one fear to another, from one worry to another. The paycheck, the marriage, the child, the house. That's all she cared about; it's all she had time for. Work mostly just got in the way. She felt lost in it all. She drove her car across the city, hoping to clear her head. She drove past the tents that lined the streets. She drove past the parks filled with homeless people. She lost herself in the traffic of her mind. She finally found herself parked outside her dad's house. She couldn't bring herself to clean it out and sell it. She thought about all the years she spent wanting to be a cop. She idolized her father and his friends when she was young. Now looking back, she felt nothing but regret. How could this be the job?

67

FIVE MONTHS LATER, KATE WAS LYING IN A HOSPITAL BED WITH A SMALL baby in her arms. Her mother fussed around the room, arranging cards and flowers that were sent to Kate from all over, it seemed. She named the baby Chance. He was a boy after all. He lay snuggled on her shoulder, breathing deeply and smelling of sweet softness. Kate was exhausted. The baby had come quickly in the night like he was in a hurry, but now he just slept on her shoulder without a care in the world.

"You just wanted to come out and say hi to everyone didn't you?" Kate said to him as she stroked his small back. His lips curled into a smile as he rocked himself back and forth.

Just then, the nurse came in and announced, "Time for someone's bath." As Kate handed him over, she mouthed the words "thank you". As the nurse left the room, Kate slipped right off the map. She awoke sometime later, and the sun was blaring through the window. She looked at her phone for the time and it said late afternoon. She read her text messages and took a deep breath to meet them. She wasn't allowed any visitors because of COVID protocols and the police detail that she still had. Her mother was the only person allowed in the hospital to see her.

She scrolled through the texts and stopped at Murdoch's. She read it and then re-read it. She put her head back and wondered where her baby was. She was hit with the same realization that she had long ago. She missed him long before she met him, and now that he was here, she wanted to be with him every second. The whole world seemed to drift away when she held him in her arms. She never had that before. He seemed to answer a lot of her questions about life: Why we are here? What is real love? What should I do with the rest of my life?

He encapsulated all those things. And he was very cute. She rubbed her sides thinking of him. It wasn't till a couple days had passed that she could head downstairs to the parking lot to see anyone. When she stepped out the doors, he was there. He was holding a big teddy bear, almost as big as him.

"Oh my God," Kate laughed. "How am I supposed to bring that upstairs?"

Murdoch pointed to her detail and said, "Get one of your henchmen to carry it up there, since they are allowed in and I'm not." He was irritated.

"Oh, be nice. I'll be home soon, and you can see him whenever you want," she smiled.

"How is he?" Murdoch said finally, hugging her in reassurance.

"He's very small and very cute," she said brimming with happiness and then she almost passed out from the emotion. He held her when she leaned forward. He patted her back as she steadied herself. Her head spun a bit. When she took her head off his chest, she took a deep breath. The baby and him smelled alike. She didn't tell him though. They talked for a few minutes, but she couldn't stay long. She needed rest. He kissed her and she swooned as she pushed him away. "They're watching," she said.

"They won't always be," he said with a smile.

As she walked into the hospital, she turned around quickly to watch him watch her, and then she exhaled and walked back in.

68

A MAN CANED HIS WAY UP BLOOR STREET IN THE TORONTO CORE. HE didn't rush. He had all night. He stopped and lit a cigarette as he looked down the street. In an alley, a block away stood a woman who had her hood pulled over her head so he could just see the gleam in her eye. She exhaled a cloud of smoke as her shape disappeared back into the darkness. 'This is too easy' he thought as he rubbed the pipe in his pocket and followed her.

THE END

CPSIA information can be obtained
at www.ICGtesting.com
Printed in the USA
BVHW050618300622
640894BV00001B/31